Out in Indian Country, a Case of Mistaken Identity Can Cost a Man His Life

Stone dropped to his knees in the soft wet mud, lowered his head, and drank from the cold clear water rippling past on its way to the great mother Mississippi.

Quick sound behind him, he turned, something whacked his head. He lost his balance, was jostled, thrown onto his back, a knife streaked toward his throat. An injun with a feather in his hair held the knife, two other injuns pinned his arms. He sucked wind as the tip of the knife touched his neck, broke the skin. A drop of blood appeared.

The injun with the knife smiled. He wore a blue bead necklace. "Ready to die, bluebelly?"

Stone struggled to break loose, but they held him in powerful muscular arms, knife point digging into striated muscle beneath his Adam's apple. "A bluebelly stole my clothes!" he protested. "You can see this uniform doesn't fit me!"

The injuns scrutinized him. Stone blurted the first words that came to mind. "I'm not a bluebelly—I fought a damned *war* against bluebellies. You want to kill a bluebelly, you better look someplace else. To hell with the bluebellies, that's what I say."

Stone smiled in a friendly manner, but the injuns observed him dispassionately. The knife remained at his throat. They were going to kill him, no question about it. . . .

• • •

SPECIAL PREVIEW!

Turn to the back of this book for a sneak-peek excerpt from the exciting, brand-new Western series . . .

FURY

. . . the blazing story of a gunfighting legend.

Also in the SEARCHER series by
Josh Edwards

SEARCHER
LYNCH LAW
TIN BADGE
WARPATH
HELLFIRE
DEVIL'S BRAND
STAMPEDE
RECKLESS GUNS

FORT HAYS BUSTOUT

Josh Edwards

DIAMOND BOOKS, NEW YORK

FORT HAYS BUSTOUT

A Diamond Book / published by arrangement
with the author

PRINTING HISTORY
Diamond edition / August 1992

ISBN 1-55773-759-2

Diamond Books are published by The Berkley Publishing Group,
200 Madison Avenue, New York, New York 10016.
The name "DIAMOND" and its logo are trademarks
belonging to Charter Communications, Inc.

PRINTED IN THE UNITED STATES OF AMERICA

10 9 8 7 6 5 4 3 2 1

FORT HAYS BUSTOUT

1

JOHN STONE LAY on the ground, coughing violently. He had pneumonia, in the midst of a vast prairie, alone and getting worse. Sweat poured off his body. His canteen was empty.

Sparse, stunted grass grew around him; it was a mild September day. His old Confederate cavalry hat hung from the pommel of his saddle. Two days ago he'd felt a mild tickle in his throat, and now he was falling apart. Tomahawk, his horse, looked at him with great concern.

Tomahawk was hobbled by rawhide. If his boss died, he'd be prisoner of anything that came along. Stone looked through bloodshot eyes at Tomahawk, the idea traveled from horse's brain to man's. Stone rolled to his knees and raised himself from the ground. His head spun, a wave of dizziness assailed him. His cheek hit the dirt.

He passed through memory and dream. A battlefield came into view, cannons fired, puffs of smoke arose from rifles. From behind a grove of trees, the Confederate cavalry charged.

They were led by a young captain with pale blond hair, sword in his right hand, yellow sash flying behind him, Stone's best friend, Ashley Tredegar. Canister ate holes in the ranks of the gray cavalrymen, but the charge thundered onward, Ashley far in front, his horse racing over the grass.

His cavalrymen galloped behind him, wind in their teeth, following their gallant young commander into the jaws of hell. Then the Union cavalrymen emerged from their position behind a hill, and their commander also had blond hair. He was twenty-four years old, the youngest general in the history of the United States Army, and told his bugler to sound the charge. The sharp bright notes pierced the tumultuous morning, as the Michigan Wolverines counterattacked across a broad front.

Cavalrymen in blue and gray galloped toward each other, whipping their swords through air filled with buzzing bullets and screaming canisters. Horses and men were ripped apart, but the Confederate cavalry plunged onward, uniforms ragged, low on ammunition, riding horses half-starved, while the onrushing Michigan Wolverines were well fed and in serviceable uniforms, their mounts the finest money could buy.

The Confederate commander's eyes glowed like red-hot coals. He was a graduate of West Point, a rich planter's son, a lover of Shakespeare and Robert Burns. The Boy General was also a West Point graduate, son of a poor farmer, his passion was war. He wore a bright crimson necktie, his eyes bright with the excitement of the charge.

The horsemen roared toward each other, officers urged their men on. Then the unthinkable happened. The young Confederate captain with pale yellow hair jerked in his saddle, his hat fell off his head. He leaned perilously to the side, and the color sergeant angled his gaunt horse toward him. Ashley Tredegar, in the first full bloom of manhood, fell out of his saddle. Men behind him tried to dodge away, but their horses' hooves trampled Ashley Tredegar into the mud and muck.

Tears came to Stone's eyes, as memories of Ashley crowded his mind. Ashley was the bravest man he ever knew, a solid loyal friend. A man like Ashley Tredegar came along once in a lifetime. It was a terrible tragic waste.

Stone spat a gob of something brown and terrible into the dirt. Life was a string of tragedies and setbacks. Nothing ever went right. A sound jogged him to awareness, he raised his eyes. Twenty Kiowa warriors rushed toward him, war hatchets in their hands!

Stone drew both his Colts, thumbed back the hammers, opened fire. Tomahawk watched in alarm as his boss aimed a barrage of hot lead into thin air. Stone got to his feet and wavered. He was six feet four, broad-shouldered, narrow at the waist. He dropped his Colts into holsters on crisscrossed belts. He had thick dark blond hair, blue eyes, and hadn't shaved in three days.

He wobbled toward Tomahawk. A giant nutcracker squeezed Stone's chest, but somehow he had to turn the faithful animal loose. He dropped to his knees before Tomahawk, reached for the hobble, his head fell onto Tomahawk's right hoof. Tomahawk looked at him sadly. Stone spun through shrouds of time. Two men faced off on the desert of New Mexico, as the sun came over the horizon. One was John Stone, and the other Beauregard Talbott, Stone's best friend in the world after Ashley Tredegar.

They drew guns, Stone was faster. He shot his old schoolboy chum in the chest. Beau lay on the ground bleeding, but Beau had forced the fight. He'd gone insane, become an outlaw, and now haunted Stone's fever dreams.

Stone sobbed deliriously. He, Ashley, and Beau had grown up together, now he was the only one left, and pneumonia had beat him to the draw. He opened his eyes. The hobbled legs of Tomahawk stood before him. Stone rose to his knees and moved toward the horse. His head felt as if it were on fire, he coughed and slobbered as he reached toward the thick bands of rawhide.

Everything went murky, he fell to his face once more. He felt alone, helpless, vulnerable. If only Marie were there to help him.

He'd grown up with her in South Carolina too, had been in love with her since he was six years old. Her face floated before him, with her high cheekbones, golden hair. She was at Fort Hays, only a day away. He'd been searching for her since the war ended, she was so close, yet so far. Marie was all he had left in the world. Somehow he had to reach her.

She was gone when he'd returned home from the war, every plantation in the county destroyed by Sherman's marauding Army. Stone's parents were dead, and neighbors told him Marie went west with a Union officer.

He'd followed her ever since, roaming the frontier like a vagabond, usually broke, drinking too much, showing her picture in every town he visited. People sent him on wild goose chases that took months to track down. He wandered long periods with no leads at all. Many times he wanted to give up, but somehow couldn't, in the grip of a love that refused to die.

Then, only a few days ago, he'd hit paydirt. An Army officer and his wife said they'd known Marie at Fort Hays, where

Stone's old West Point classmate Fannie Custer was commanding officer. They said Marie was married to the provost marshal, Bob Scanlon.

Now he was on his way to Fort Hays, but might not make it. Illness was eating him alive. He'd never been so sick in his life, except for when he'd been wounded in the war. But he had to find Marie.

She had a lot of questions to answer, and they tormented him along with his fever and the knot in his stomach. How could she run away without leaving a message? Why couldn't she wait until he returned home? Had she stopped loving him?

He raised his eyes, and she stood above him, dressed in a brown coat. "Marie," he whispered, reaching for her hand. Her face disappeared, replaced by Tomahawk's snout.

Stone snapped awake. He took a deep breath, coughed, was attacked by the dry heaves. He focused all his remaining reserves of energy and willed himself to unclasp the hobble.

Tomahawk stepped free. No saddle on his back, he could run away, but couldn't leave now that Stone cared enough to set him loose.

Tomahawk took a few steps back and watched solemnly as Stone hugged himself to keep warm. The sun was setting, and Stone felt like a block of ice. The only thing to do was light a fire. He'd rather be shot by an injun than die from the cold.

He gathered buffalo chips, struck a match against a rock, lit a fire, and huddled against it, teeth chattering.

Tomahawk stared at the endless rolling prairie. Great herds of wild horses were out there, he could join them, but he'd been born on a ranch and raised by cowboys. He knew no other life, and felt a strange connection to the tormented man at the fire, rubbing himself frantically, the Apache blanket wrapped around him. Tomahawk would stay till he died, then join the wild ones.

"I smell smoke," said Private Snead, wearing a blue Army uniform with the insignia torn off.

"Might be injuns," replied Private Gotcher.

They sat upon Army saddles and horses, pulled back Army reins, deserters on their way to the gold fields of Colorado. Snead was slim, with a narrow face. Gotcher was on the heavy side, brown stubble on his cheeks. Both joined the Army for the free trip west, they never had any intention of being soldiers. Gotcher was wanted for armed robbery in Ohio. Snead shot a policeman in Baltimore. They teamed up at Fort Dodge, and went over the hill together.

"Smell it too," Gotcher said, twitching his round red nose. "We best steer clear of it."

"Might be a couple dumb cowboys, we can take 'em by surprise." Snead drew his gun. "Git their money and rifles."

"What if it's injuns?"

"We'll see 'em long afore they see us."

"I ain't lookin' fer an arrow in me gullet," Gotcher said. "Count me out."

"Need money and civilian clothes. Got to take chances."

"Not me." Gotcher raised his hand. "Guess we come to the fork in the road."

"That's the way you feel about it . . ."

Gotcher turned toward Colorado, and the sleek cavalry mount plodded away. Snead lowered his hand to his gun. If Gotcher got caught, he might spill the beans, tell the Army where to look.

Snead drew his gun, thumbed back the hammer, *click*. Gotcher heard the sound, turned his head in surprise. A shot reverberated across the plains. Gotcher felt as though a mule team rammed into his back. He was thrown against his horse's mane, then sagged to the ground.

He rolled onto his back and looked at Snead, who was aiming for a second shot.

"Should've knowed . . . you was a backshooter," Gotcher gasped.

"But you didn't," Snead replied, pulling the trigger.

Ray Slipchuck, old stagecoach driver of the plains, opened his eyes in the Drovers Cottage, Abilene. The final orange rays of the setting sun slanted into the room, falling upon the face of the young prostitute sleeping next to him.

She'd been expensive, but worth every penny. Her skin was smooth and unblemished, like the finest silk. It wasn't every day an old ruin like Slipchuck could sleep with a young woman, but he'd just been paid after three long months on the trail with a herd of Texas longhorns.

He gazed at her profile. She sure gave him a run for his money, did every weird degraded stunt concocted by his warped, lonely old man's mind. They even did it on the floor like dogs. But now Slipchuck felt more dead than alive. His age finally caught up with him.

The young prostitute opened her eyes, in yet another hotel room. Her life was an endless series of them. Who was the guy this time? She rolled toward him, saw a toothless geezer. He smelled like tobacco and whiskey, looked like a mongrel wire-haired terrier.

"Howdy," he said, tossing a little salute.

She remembered him now, but she'd had worse, like the traveling salesman who tied her to the bed.

"I was figgerin' we could git us some grub," Slipchuck said.

"Got to go home," she replied.

With sinking heart, he watched her dress. Bit by bit her luscious body was covered by her red gown.

"How's about tonight?" Slipchuck said.

"We'll see," she replied in a perfunctory way, and Slipchuck remembered when he was young, he didn't always have to pay.

"How's about a good-bye kiss?" he asked hopefully.

"You already got yer kisses, old man. Should be in the clink fer the thangs you made me do." She smiled, blew him a kiss. "Maybe some other time, hey, cowboy?"

"I'll be a-lookin' fer you at the Lone Star."

She left the room. He felt old, tired, defeated. But an old stagecoach driver has to keep clicking off the miles. If he lingered in Abilene, he might miss John Stone, his pardner, at Fort Hays.

Slipchuck inhaled the fragrance of the pillow where the whore's mahogany locks had lain. If only . . .

Tomahawk fidgeted, someone was coming. His ears pricked up and he gazed in the direction of the sound. Help or trouble, hard to know. He moved next to Stone and prodded him with his snout, but Stone was out like a light. The rider drew closer, and Tomahawk didn't want to get caught. He trotted away, where he could watch from the distance.

Snead heard muffled hoofbeats, but didn't know if they were his imagination, the wind, a tribe of bloodthirsty injuns, or bluebellies tracking him down. He pulled back his horse's reins, listened, but the sound didn't repeat. Tomahawk stood quietly in the shadows. Snead thought it was the wind. A man's ears played tricks on him.

He'd seen the glowing embers of the fire from a hogback in the distance, and homed in on it. Didn't look like injuns, but his regulation Colt .45 was cocked, ready in hand. He climbed from his horse, hobbled it, and moved toward the fire.

He came to a small clearing, where a solitary man slept beside the ashes. Snead crept forward, as Tomahawk watched the gun in his hand. Stone felt something cold against his forehead.

"Git up real slow," Snead said, "keep yer hands where I can see 'em."

Stone wondered if this were a hallucination like all the others. He reached forward to touch Snead, who slammed the gun against Stone's head. Stone's eyes rolled up as he collapsed onto the ground.

Snead undressed him, put on his clothes, took his twin Colts and gunbelts, rifle, saddle, money, even his Confederate cavalry hat. It was on the big side, but might be good for a free drink in a saloon full of Texas cowboys. He threw the regulation Colt and bayonet to the ground, not wanting anything that might identify him as a deserter.

He found the picture of Marie in the shirt pocket, tossed it over his shoulder. He wished he could get his hands on the cowboy's horse, but the animal kept his distance. "C'mon, boy," Snead said, pretending to have a lump of sugar in his hand. "I got somethin' nice fer you."

Tomahawk didn't fall for it. Snead put Stone's saddle and bedroll on his stolen Army horse, planning to rob the first civilian horse he found. Stone lay naked on the ground, Snead's clothes and Army blanket nearby.

Snead was ready to leave. He raised the gun to Stone's head. Why waste a bullet on a dying cowboy? He climbed onto his horse and rode away, Stone's cavalry hat on the back of his head.

Tomahawk waited until he was out of earshot, then emerged from the shadows. He caught the Army blanket in his teeth and spread it over the naked man wheezing through a clogged and swollen throat. Tomahawk stood guard nearby, chomping grass, swishing his tail nervously.

2

STONE SHIVERED AND burned. He threw the blanket off, pulled it on again. Coughing, hacking, spitting, he passed the night.

He gained consciousness, his body a massive hurt, barely able to think. He'd lost weight, cheeks hollowed, eyes bloodshot. He saw the uniform nearby, arose laboriously, put it on. It was much too small, the trousers halfway to his knees, but a man couldn't be naked on the cold prairie. His eyes fell on Marie's picture, he bent to pick it up, and passed out again. He hit the ground, and Tomahawk covered him with the Army blanket.

Stone drifted into phantasmagorical nightmares. Tomahawk took his position as guard. Another long night of dangerous possibilities lay ahead.

Slipchuck rode through the tall gateposts of Fort Hays, and the Army post stretched before him, parade ground surrounded by wooden buildings. Enlisted men in one section, married officers in another, headquarters building straight ahead, flag of the Seventh Cavalry fluttering in the breeze.

A group of mounted cavalrymen approached, led by a young lieutenant with his campaign hat slanted low over his eyes. The lieutenant touched his finger to the brim as Slipchuck approached.

Slipchuck turned in the saddle, looked at the officer, ramrod straight, red hair, tanned, spiffy. "Bet he gets lots of girls," Slipchuck muttered.

He came to the headquarters building, climbed down Buckshot, threw the reins over the rail, hitched up his gun. He strolled past soldiers standing guard on either side of door, and for all they knew, he might have ten pounds dynamite tucked into his shirt.

Slipchuck was lean, five and a half feet tall, and had been nearly everywhere, done just about everything. A gruff master sergeant with a face like a bulldog looked up from his desk. *Another civilian to screw up my day.*

Slipchuck took off his hat. A large portrait of President Grant hung on one wall, the head of a buffalo mounted on the other. The office was spotless, and Slipchuck knew who kept it that way.

"I'm supposed to meet a feller name of John Stone here," Slipchuck said. "He check in yet?"

"Never heard of 'im."

The sergeant returned to the paperwork on his desk; Slipchuck headed for the door. *Johnny should be here by now. Hope the injuns didn't get him.*

It was dark on the prairie, Tomahawk smelled lobos in the breeze, and heard their yelps in the distance. They'd found the rotting corpse of Gotcher, and Tomahawk hoped they wouldn't drift in his direction. John Stone was helpless, Tomahawk couldn't handle a pack of lobos himself, but he'd try.

Tomahawk lowered his head and looked through large luminous eyes at Stone, who breathed noisily on the ground. Stone had tremendous powers of endurance when sober, but had been drunk most of the past six months.

Lobos howled in the distance. Tomahawk was tired, hungry, thirsty, spooked. He hoped Stone would come around soon.

The Tumbleweed Saloon was thick with smoke and conversation. Soldiers, civilians and whores swilled down whiskey, while against the far wall, a man in a striped shirt and arm garters sat at a piano and plunked a tune.

Slipchuck made his way to the bar, hand near his Colt; a man could never tell when a bad penny from his past might show up. Two feet of space were available between two soldiers, and Slipchuck sidled in.

"Whiskey," he said to the bartender.

Slipchuck rolled a cigarette, and checked the lay of the land. Mounted on the far wall was a cavalry sword, and near it a homemade 7th Cavalry flag. A young freckle-faced soldier stood to Slipchuck's left, staring into his empty glass.

"Fill 'er up?" asked the bartender.

"No more money," the soldier said sadly, with an Irish brogue.

"Bartender," Slipchuck said, "give this soldier a whiskey on me, if you don't mind."

The bartender filled the glass, and the soldier raised it to his lips. He drained half the liquid, then wiped his mouth with the back of his hand. "Don't believe I got your name," he said with a burr on his tongue.

"Slipchuck. You ain't been in America long, I don't guess."

"Six months, most of 'em in the Seventh Cavalry. Five years to go, and by the great snappin'-toed Jesus, don't think I'll make it." He lifted the glass and drained it dry. "Name's O'Reilly."

Anybody stationed at Fort Hays was a potential source of information about John Stone's former girlfriend, Marie. Slipchuck thought he'd gather information for his pard, and also satisfy his own curiosity about the woman who made John Stone tick.

"You know who Marie Scanlon is?" he asked.

"Sure I do. Wife of Major Scanlon."

"What's she like?"

"You must be new around here."

"Just showed up. Supposed to meet my pard here, name of John Stone. He's a-lookin' fer her."

"Tell him to keep on lookin'. She ain't here no more."

"Where'd she go?"

"Your guess is as good as mine."

"She go alone?"

"A woman like that don't do nothin' alone. She run off with Derek Canfield, the gambler."

Slipchuck gazed into a dark corner, where two whores fondled a drunken corporal. Did Johnny find out about Marie's departure and follow her? Maybe he went on a drunk, or shot himself. The man was crazy where that woman was concerned. Private O'Reilly, having drained the contents of his glass, placed it loudly on the bar.

"Another whiskey for my friend," Slipchuck instructed the bartender.

As the bartender filled the glass, a loud argument brok
on the far side of the room. O'Reilly lifted his glass. "Wh
I ever leave the old sod?" He slurped an inch off the top.
the whiskey don't get me, Custer will. I wish somebody'd pu
a bullet in that goddamn poppycock's head."

"I'll drink to that," said the trooper to the left of O'Reilly. He had tanned cheeks, and the front brim of his campaign hat was turned up. Everyone touched glasses.

"What's wrong with Custer?" Slipchuck asked. "Heard he was a good man."

"Good for what?" asked O'Reilly. "Treats his huntin' dogs better'n us."

"Hate the son of a bitch," said the other trooper. "You want a good general, that's George Crook. He knows a man has to eat and sleep. Old Iron Butt jest looks after his pals at headquarters. Like the man said, somebody's gonna shoot that son of a bitch someday."

Slipchuck motioned to the bartender, who poured another round. The three men drank, then the trooper introduced himself: "Amos Thatcher."

"You know Marie Scanlon?"

"Don't care what they say about her. I always thought she was all right."

"What they say about her?"

"Worst bitch in the world. Screwed all the officers. Don't give a shit about nobody. Drove her husband to drink. Run off with Derek Canfield, the gambler."

"You ever see him?"

"Used to play cards right in here. Tall skinny galoot, looked like death warmed over, but no accountin' fer taste. Had me a little talk with Marie Scanlon onc't, few months back. Was on a police detail near her house, she was in her backyard. Asked where I was from, said she grew up in the South, missed the trees and flowers more'n anything else. Had the feelin' she was lonely."

O'Reilly grinned. "You should've gone inside and slipped it to 'er."

"She was a lady."

"Ladies like it more'n anybody else."

Slipchuck scratched his beard. The more he listened, the

worse it sounded. When Johnny found out, he'd rip the town apart. Where the hell was he anyway?

Tomahawk was thirsty. Coyotes howled in the distance. The last water was a half-day back, but Tomahawk didn't want to leave John Stone undefended. Yet if Tomahawk didn't get water soon, he'd die too.

He had to go. Better one survivor than none. He looked at Stone lying on the ground, wrapped in his blanket. Maybe the coyotes wouldn't find him. Either way, Tomahawk needed water.

He touched his thick lips to Stone's hair, and wished him well. *We've covered many miles together, friend.* Then Tomahawk turned toward the last water, pain and sorrow in his heart.

The lobo watched from behind a mesquite bush, eyes glittering like diamonds. The man in the blanket looked dead or close to it as the horse plodded off into the night. The prairie became still. The lobo focused his ears and held his breath. He could hear the man breathing through his clogged throat—alive, but not by much.

The lobo feasted on carrion that night, but there was always room for more. Quivering with excitement, licking his chops, he crawled toward the man wrapped in the blanket.

John Stone dreamed of a gala plantation party at the beginning of the war. Crystal chandeliers sparkled above the ballroom floor as he held Marie's hands and twirled her among the other dancers.

Marie wore a maroon velvet hoop skirt and a white silk blouse with a jade heart over her breast, while Stone had on his new gray Confederate officer's uniform. The fragrance of magnolia blossoms drifted through open windows, and the crescent moon rested near the tops of trees. He gazed into her shimmering blue eyes.

"I wish you didn't have to go away, Johnny."

"Be back before you know it. Yankees'll leave us alone once we bloody their noses a few times."

"You'll meet other girls, and they'll fall all over you. You'll forget me."

"I'll never forget you, Marie. I'll love you till the day I die. You're the only girl for me."

She smiled, and the fetid odor of carrion rose from her lips. He opened his eyes. Only inches away was a lobo, fangs glittering in the moonlight.

The lobo lunged for his throat, and Stone raised his arm to protect himself. The lobo's teeth sank into Stone's wrist, the sudden violent pain bringing him to total consciousness. He screamed as his final reserves of adrenaline dumped into his bloodstream.

The lobo hung on, eyes emitting sparks of light, growling and howling, calling his compadres. Stone jumped to his feet, but the lobo clamped down tenaciously. Stone grabbed the lobo's throat with his free hand and squeezed, forcing the lobo to loosen his hold on Stone's arm.

Stone flung him to the ground, but the lobo landed on his paws, turned around and snarled. Stone's heart chugged in his chest, blood rushed past his ears, he was light-headed, dizzy—where was Tomahawk? He heard coyotes yipping and yelling as they rushed toward him over the grass.

Stone looked for a weapon, but saw nothing other than his bare hands. The lobo stood before him, growling and spitting, tensed to strike as soon as the others arrived.

They sped toward him and called out to each other in the thrill of the chase. Killing was their greatest pleasure, they could taste fresh blood on their tongues. Ahead in the shadows their brother held the man at bay. The lobos shrieked with delight as they charged in for the kill.

Stone wheeled to meet them with his bare hands. They dived onto him all at once, their sharp pointed teeth bared. He kicked, spun, slammed them with his fists, performing his dance of death in the moonlight. The lobos sensed his weakness and knew it was just a matter of time. They lunged again, sinking their teeth into his flesh.

He tore a lobo off his arm and flung it howling and twisting through the air. Another lobo flew toward his throat, but when he punched it in the jaw, it fell unconscious to the ground. Another lobo dug his teeth into the ankle of Stone's left boot, and Stone stomped on his head with his big right boot, crushing his skull.

Another jumped Stone from behind, digging his teeth deeply into Stone's ass. Stone jumped three feet into the air as two more lobos dived onto his left leg. He lost his balance and fell to the ground, where lobos swarmed over him, tearing his flesh. He dodged, whacked, elbowed, tried to shake them loose. Finally his eyes fell on something gleaming dully in the grass—the bayonet left by the Army deserter.

Stone scooped it up, whirled, lashed out, and the blade caught a lobo's throat. Two lobos sailed through the air at him, and three more attacked from his rear. He dodged and whipped the knife, tearing an angry red gash across the coat of one lobo, then rammed the blade into another lobo's mouth.

A third lobo clamped his jaws onto Stone's forearm. Stone jammed the bayonet to the hilt into the lobo's belly, ripping it wide open. The remaining lobos realized he wouldn't be as easy as they'd thought, and weren't hungry enough to continue. They howled defiantly as they backed away.

Stone stood unsteadily on legs far apart, his body covered with lobo bites, the bloody bayonet in his fist. "You want a fight, I'll give you a fight!"

Lobos wanted food, not a fight. Snarling, bodies trembling with tension, they retreated farther into the darkness. *We'll, wait till you drop.*

The night swallowed them up; Stone was alone with bleeding gashes and the saliva of lobos staining his blue uniform. He sucked the cool night air into his lungs and waited in case the lobos tried a sneak attack.

Where was Tomahawk? His faithful horse had deserted him, and Stone guessed the reason: water. He gazed at dead lobos on the ground, but knew they'd get him in the end. He was sick, weak, feverish, adrenaline wearing off, mouth dry, stomach cavernous. He needed nourishment desperately.

Blood glistened in the moonlight. Stone knelt before the lobo with the slashed throat, fastened his lips to the open wound, and sucked salty blood. It had a wild doggy taste, but Stone swallowed it down. He sat on the ground, butchered the lobo, and sliced off a steak. It was stringy, dreadful, and smelly, but food. His jaws ached as he chewed the tough meat, blood dripping down his chin, staining his fingers.

Fatigue fell over him as he wiped his mouth with the back of his sleeve. Nightbirds squawked in the distance, stars emblazoned the sky. Dead lobos would attract wildcats. *Best get moving.*

He pulled himself to his feet, saw a blanket, the Army saddle,

Army uniform, bayonet, and regulation revolver with no bullets. *Take the saddle?* He picked it up, but couldn't carry it far. It was difficult enough to carry himself.

He affixed the bayonet scabbard to the belt and jammed the gun into the holster. Onto his head he dropped the too-small campaign hat, and missed his old Confederate cavalry hat, his good luck charm. He'd been through five years of war with it, now it was gone. He felt weaker somehow, and Fort Hays was twenty miles away. He looked to the sky and found the Big Dipper and the North Star. Fort Hays was in a northwesterly direction, so he tilted in that direction.

Something bright and shiny on the ground caught his attention. He bent over and saw Marie's picture. Dropping to his knees, he picked it up.

Marie gazed at him. *Don't give up now.* He tucked the picture into his shirt pocket, buttoned the flap, and staggered across the prairie, following the stars. Behind him, lobos howled as they devoured those Stone had killed.

One foot in front of the other. March or die. He heard lobos on his trail, growling low in their throats. As soon as he fell, he knew, they'd be all over him. The bitter taste of lobo blood was on his tongue. His ears felt long, pointed toward the stars. The prairie was drenched with death. He raised his face to the starry heavens and howled like a lobo.

Slipchuck checked the jail, but Stone wasn't there. It was three o'clock in the morning, and Slipchuck was at a table in the Tumbleweed Saloon wondering what to do. He only had thirty dollars left out of the hundred he'd been paid after the drive. He'd have to slow down, start thinking about a job. Maybe forgo a hotel for the night and sleep on the ground like a man.

A few civilian drunks and whores were the only ones left in the saloon. All the soldiers had returned to the fort, where they had to stand reveille in a few hours.

A young Mexican whore dropped into a chair at Slipchuck's table. "What you say, papi?" she asked in her south-of-the-border accent. "Want to go upstairs?" She had dark flashing eyes and a fine profile.

"Not in the mood," Slipchuck said.

She raised her eyebrows. "Do not geeve me that sheet. You

lie through your teeth. You do not have the money, go ahead and say eet."

"It's true, I don't have much left in my poke. I git a job, be back to see you."

She looked at him seductively. "Eet ees late at night. Beeziness ees slow. For only eight pesos you come to my room for the whole night." She unbuttoned the front of her gown and peeled back the fabric.

He gazed at her ripe young breasts. She couldn't be more than twenty. What the hell was eight dollars?

"You got yoreself a deal," Slipchuck said. "Just let me finish my drink." He raised his glass of whiskey. "Want one?"

"Sí, señor."

Slipchuck brought two glasses of whiskey back to the table, trying to walk steady like a young man, not like the arthritic disaster he really was.

He sat opposite her. "Been in Hays City long?"

"Few months."

"Ever hear of Marie Scanlon?"

The whore smiled. "La Rubia, I know who she ees. I have even see her weeth my own eyes. What ees she to you?"

"Friend of mine's lookin' fer her. What's she like?"

"A man weel shoot her someday, because she does what she wants, like me." The whore laughed. "Let's go to bed, papi. I show you a good time."

John Stone shuffled across the prairie, lobos following twenty feet behind. If he fell, they'd pounce. He had to keep going. Marie was waiting for him at Fort Hays. If he could find a water hole, he'd be all right.

Instead he found a gopher hole; his leg dropped down halfway to his knee, and he pitched forward onto his face before he could raise his hands for protection. The lobos rushed forward, thinking he'd finally gone down, but he smashed one in the mouth with a backhand swing, then slammed another in the eye.

Stone got to his feet, pulled his bayonet. "Let's see what you've got," he said to them. He beckoned, a growl in his throat. They looked at each other, then stepped back. He still had strength, they'd have to wait a while longer.

Stone looked at the sky and found his direction. He stumbled toward Fort Hays, mouth dry, boots dragging over the grass. *Keep going and don't even think about stopping.*

Rosita slept on her back, hands folded neatly on her belly. Slipchuck held the covers up with his bony arm, gazed at her voluptuous naked body in the moonlight.

He felt better with her asleep, because she couldn't see his aged flesh, wrinkled knees, gray hair, pouches under the eyes, no teeth, the list went on endlessly. But in the darkness he could pretend he was a young stagecoach driver again, and all the pretty girls were in love with him.

That's the way it was in the old days. He'd walked into the stagecoach station, the owner came and shook his hand, nothing too good for him. Pretty girls from the East had been fascinated with him. He still loved them same as he always did, but now they saw him as a funny-looking old billygoat.

Rosita opened her eyes. "I am cold, papi. Geeve me the blankets."

He dropped them over her, snuggled, closed his eyes. She felt warm and fabulously alive against his withered flesh. Thank you, Jesus.

Stone saw the first dim glimmer of dawn, and thought his eyes were playing tricks. He'd hallucinated everything from injuns to monster bears in the course of the night.

He stopped, took his bearings. If he were lucky he'd run into a stagecoach or troop of cavalry on patrol. He turned. Thirteen lobos trailed behind him, watching patiently. Stone drew the bayonet. "Come on, you sons of bitches!"

They didn't move. When he collapsed, they'd eat him. Simple as that. He put the bayonet away. The sun was a red-orange sliver on the horizon. A stream wound like a long thin snake in the distance. If he could reach it, he'd survive.

The sun rose in the sky, and the stream came into sharper focus, lined by green grass and willows. Anticipation gave him strength, his feet came down more firmly. If a man keeps plugging away, he'll be all right.

Lobos whined and sniveled as they followed like ardent suitors. They still hoped he might fall into their jaws. A prairie dog raised his head out of his burrow and looked at Stone, who threw him a West Point salute. *I'm at my best when I live like a soldier.*

The stream came closer, his pace quickened. He breathed deeply, felt strength returning, outlasted pneumonia, survived a robbery, fought coyotes. He came to the edge of the stream, looked toward the ground, saw no tracks. Once he'd stumbled onto a bear beside a stream, never do it again. He wished he had bullets for his gun. The deserter would pay with his life, if they ever met again.

It was cool in the willows, the stream ten feet wide, clear as crystal. Stone held his bayonet ready for anything. If only he had one measly bullet. The grass inclined toward the water. Lobos moaned and drooled behind him. They wondered whether to search for a more promising meal. Something moved on the ground ahead, they stopped in their tracks, twitched noses nervously.

Stone didn't notice their retreat, his eyes on the cold clear water rippling past on its way to the great mother Mississippi. He dropped to his knees in the soft wet mud, lowered his head, drank.

He felt better immediately, would get sick if he overdid it. He threw the campaign hat to the side, scooped water in his hands, splashed it over his face. Quick sound behind him, he turned, something whacked his head. He lost his balance, was jostled, thrown onto his back, a knife streaked toward his throat. An injun with a feather in his hair held the knife, two other injuns pinned his arms. He sucked wind as the tip of the knife touched his neck, broke the skin. A drop of blood appeared.

The injun with the knife smiled. He wore a blue bead necklace. "Ready to die, bluebelly?"

Stone tried to break loose, they held him in powerful muscular arms, knife point digging into striated muscle beneath his Adam's apple. "A bluebelly stole my clothes!" he protested. "You can see this uniform doesn't fit me!"

The injuns scrutinized him. They were mid-twenties, dressed in buckskin, armed to the teeth. Stone's sleeves and pants too short, buttons burst on the fly, fabric stretched to the limit, seams coming undone. He blurted the first words that came to mind. "I'm not a bluebelly—I fought a damned *war* against bluebellies. You want to kill a bluebelly, you'd better look someplace else. To hell with the bluebellies, that's what I say."

Stone smiled in a friendly manner, but the injuns observed

him dispassionately. The knife remained at his throat, they were going to kill him, no question about it.

"I used to be a warrior too," he said, and went into a paroxysm of coughing. "At least give me a fighting chance. How'd you like to get your throat cut like a chicken? Let me die like a man."

The injuns looked at each other. One of them said something, they let him go. Stone rose to his feet, while lobos watched eagerly from the distance. Looked like another meal in the offing.

Stone reached for his bayonet, but the injuns already had taken it and his empty gun. He raised his fists and bent his legs. The injuns stared at the bedraggled teetering white man covered with scars, blood, fresh coyote bites, wearing ridiculous clothing. He could barely hold himself erect.

"Come on, you devils!" Stone hollered, brandishing his fists. He charged one of the injuns, who dodged to the side. Stone faced the wide-open prairie. The injun's chortled behind his back.

He spun around, grit his teeth, held up his fists. "You can laugh all you want, but just let me get my hands on you!"

He rushed them, one stuck out his foot, Stone sprawled nose first into the stream. He rolled over, coughing and sputtering, while the injuns roared with mirth.

"You don't have the guts to stand up to a real man!" Stone said hoarsely. He snarled and rushed another warrior, who didn't run away. Stone threw a punch at the injun's face, but the injun made a strange fast move. Stone was thrown to the ground before he knew what hit him.

The injun looked at him. "I can see you have a warrior's heart. I will not kill you this day."

Stone's eyes were like saucers. The injun who'd spoken pulled Stone's gun out of his belt, handed it back.

Stone took it. The injun scooped bullets out of a leather pouch, dropped six into the palm of Stone's hand. Then he handed back the bayonet. Stone thought he was dreaming. It wasn't supposed to happen this way. His wet scalp should be hanging from the injuns belt right now.

"I'd like to know your name," Stone said.

"I am Black Wing. That is Yellow Bear, and here is Many Horses."

"I'm John Stone. You speak good English. You've been to one of our schools?"

"I had the white man's education, but the white man preaches one thing and does another."

"I don't preach anything," Stone replied, "because I don't know anything." He put on the campaign hat, it was too small and perched comically atop his head.

Black Wing opened the leather pouch on his belt, took out a chunk of jerked buffalo meat. "Want to eat, John Stone?"

Stone gnawed the meat ravenously. They sat in a circle on the ground. Yellow Beaver tossed Stone a U.S. Cavalry canteen, probably taken from a dead trooper. Stone looked at the savages smeared with war paint, and wanted to ask why they mutilated enemies, but it wouldn't be the best diplomatic move. He wondered how they lived, what were their hopes and dreams. He'd spent a few days with Apaches, but not long enough to learn much. The warriors offered him another chunk of jerked meat.

Black Wing stiffened suddenly. Yellow Bear looked toward the east. Many Horses rose to his feet. "Somebody coming."

Tomahawk trudged across the prairie, head hanging low. He'd been following John Stone's trail since the middle of the night, and found the spot where Stone fought the lobos, while buzzards feasted merrily on the dead. Tomahawk studied Stone's footprint, and saw the times he'd faltered. But he kept going. Tomahawk had seen Stone survive gunfights, injun attacks, shootouts, showdowns, knife wars, and every other conceivable type of violence and mayhem. The man attracted trouble as a whirlpool pulls fallen leaves into its swirling vortex.

Tomahawk saw the stream from afar, pulled toward it steadily. Good to be without a saddle, like a colt again, moving free instead of at the bidding of a man drunk most of the time. They'd been in scrapes where both had nearly been killed due to Stone's drunkenness.

Cautiously, Tomahawk approached the stream. He knew that other men would want him, but couldn't get caught. He sniffed faint trace of jerked buffalo. He stopped and pricked up his ears, scanned the area with big brown eyes, but saw no strange shapes, everything was still. He advanced stealthily, a proud beast with large hooves, lines of a plow horse, plenty of bottom. Stone's trail led to the water, followed by the lobos, who now watched from afar, hoping someone would get slaughtered.

Grass lay flat straight ahead, and Tomahawk slowed. What had done that? He smelled men's sweat. Stone's trail became confused. What had happened here?

The grass burst forth in multiple explosions, Tomahawk reared backward. Three injuns and John Stone jumped out of the ground! Tomahawk ran away.

"Hey, Tomahawk!" Stone shouted. "It's me!"

Tomahawk looked back over his shoulder. It was the boss, all right.

"It's okay! C'mere!"

Tomahawk stared at them laughing. It was an astonishing spectacle. Tomahawk whinnied nervously as he walked toward John Stone.

"This is Tomahawk," Stone said. "Best damn horse I ever owned."

Tomahawk's chest swelled with pride. The injuns looked him over approvingly.

"I will make you a hackamore," Black Wing said. He removed a ball of rawhide from a U.S. Army regulation haversack stolen from a disemboweled trooper, measured it against Tomahawk's head, made knots, adjusted the hackamore into place, handed Stone the reins.

Stone led Tomahawk to the stream and let him drink. Black Wing gave Stone a handful of jerked buffalo meat and a U.S. Army canteen. Stone stuffed the jerky between his skin and the shirt, draped the canteen strap over his shoulder.

"You are welcome to return with us, to our tents," Black Wing said.

"Can't," Stone replied. "There's a woman . . ."

"There is always a woman."

Stone shook their hands. "Perhaps another time . . ."

"Ask for Black Wing among the Sioux. They all know the son of Elk Thunder."

Stone had heard the name. Elk Thunder was a fighting chief of the Lakota tribe. The three warriors weren't ordinary run-of-the-mill wild bucks, but the injun aristocracy. They helped Stone onto Tomahawk's bare back, and Stone pointed the animal toward Fort Hays. The three warriors watched him ride away in his tight, too-short uniform, hat hanging perilously atop his head.

"He is a holy fool," Black Wing said. "The Great Spirit will surely take care of him."

Slipchuck entered the orderly room. Sergeant Major Gillespie sat behind his desk, reading morning reports. He didn't glance up as Slipchuck approached nervously.

"I was a-wonderin' if that feller John Stone showed up here yet," Slipchuck said, fingering the brim of his hat.

The sergeant continued his perusal of morning reports. "Ain't been here."

Slipchuck retreated from the orderly room. The sun was high in the sky. Soldiers drilled on the parade ground. Other soldiers dug holes, repaired buildings, painted, swept, washed, and cleaned. Typical morning at a fort, Slipchuck had seen a million of them.

He sat on a bench nestled against the wall of the orderly room, wondered what to do. What happened to John Stone? Had he followed Marie, leaving his pard behind? Did he blow his brains out in a barn? Maybe he was drunk in an alley.

Slipchuck couldn't wait indefinitely. At some point he'd have to get a job, not a simple prospect for an older man. If push came to shove, he'd go back to the Triangle Spur Ranch in Texas.

A group of men and women riders entered the front gate of the fort. At their front, atop a sideways-prancing black horse, sat a man in a fringed buckskin jacket and pants, wearing a wide-brimmed black hat, long gold curls falling to his shoulders. Slipchuck got to his feet. It was Custer.

The riders drew closer. Custer was tall and erect on his horse, head high, the great conquering hero of the Union Army who had led the crucial cavalry charge at Gettysburg. Beside him rode his woman, pretty, with voluminous skirts, campaign hat low over her eyes.

Behind them came officers and wives returning from a morning ride on the prairie, with an armed escort. Slipchuck stared at Custer bouncing up and down atop his horse. So that was him. The great man himself. From the rear, with his long golden hair, he looked almost like a woman.

Hardscrabble farm in the middle of the prairie, dugout house with roof built onto the ground. A woman in a dirty dress and bonnet came out the front door, shielding her eyes from the sun with gnarled hands.

"Howdy," Stone said, climbing down from Tomahawk. "You got some water for my canteen?"

The woman looked at him suspiciously. "Spring's in back."

Stone led Tomahawk to the rear of the house, found the spring next to a pole with a bucket, tin cup hanging from a nail. Stone filled the bucket for Tomahawk, then kneeled beside the spring and dipped in the cup.

The water was cold and clear, he could see all the way to the bottom, white sand dancing. He raised the cup to his lips, water sweet and pure dribbled down his throat.

"Hold it right thar, deserter!" said a voice behind him.

Stone turned around. A man in ragged clothes and tattered hat stood with his legs spread apart, shotgun aimed at Stone's belly. "I'm not a deserter," Stone said. "I'm a civilian. Deserter stole my clothes."

"Tell it to the judge. Git his gun, Sally Mae."

The woman pulled the Colt out of Stone's Army holster.

"Git back on yer horse, deserter," the man said. "You an' me—we're a-takin' a leetle ride."

Slipchuck entered the Tumbleweed Saloon, nearly deserted in the early afternoon. He ordered a whiskey, carried it to a table against the wall, sat, pushed his hat back on his head.

John Stone surely would've left a message if he'd passed on. Something must've happened to him. Slipchuck wondered whether to backtrack, see if he could find him.

An old whore dropped into the chair next to him, wearing a low-cut dress that revealed a substantial portion of her pudgy, wrinkled anatomy. "Buy me a drink?" she asked hopefully.

"What's yer pleasure?"

"Whiskey."

Slipchuck called the waitress, gave the order, then returned to the whore. "How long you been in Hays City?"

"Two years."

"Know Marie Scanlon?"

"Wouldn't 'zactly say she was a friend of mine, but I knew who she was."

"My pard was supposed to marry her."

"If there's any woman who ain't the marryin' kind, it's Marie

Scanlon. I'd tell him find somebody else, I was you."

"Heard she run off with Derek Canfield the gambler. You ever meet him?"

"Came here all the time. Smart feller, had a smile fer everybody, but I wouldn't mess with him. Marie Scanlon was a regular little spitfire. Cheated on her husband with Lieutenant Forrest too, and they say she even crawled onto the bedspread with Custer hisself."

Stone rode through the gates of Fort Hays, lights glowed in the barracks. His arms were bound behind his back, Amos Tillet rode beside him, shotgun cradled in his arms.

Stone was sure he could straighten the matter out soon as he spoke with the man in charge. The worst part was nearly over, the sodbuster with the shotgun hadn't blown his head off by mistake on the ride to the fort.

He looked at officers' row, the command post, armory, barracks. He'd been an officer five years, but spent most of his service in the field, sleeping in tents when lucky, usually making a bed on the ground. The guardhouse was a squat building with barred windows behind the stable, fragrance of manure heavy in the air. Amos Tillet climbed down from his horse, threw the reins over the rail, pointed his shotgun at Stone. "Git down."

Stone swung his leg over Tomahawk's back, and jumped to the ground.

"Walk toward that door. Make one wrong move, I'll blow yer fuckin' head off."

"Easy on that trigger," Stone replied calmly, so as not to rile him.

Tomahawk watched them approach the door. Stone hadn't bothered to tie the hackamore to the rail, and Amos Tillet hadn't noticed. Tomahawk could slip the hackamore easily and run away. It was night, no one would see him. Tomahawk didn't want any part of the U.S. Cavalry. The door to the guardhouse opened, Stone and Tillet went inside.

Tomahawk lowered his head, tangled reins in his hooves, yanked back his neck. The hackamore fell to the ground. Tomahawk moved into the shadows and headed toward the open prairie.

Inside the guardhouse, Corporal Warwick looked Stone over

sternly in the light of the lantern on his desk. "What outfit were you with, deserter?"

"I'm a civilian. A deserter robbed me, took my clothes, left his. I finally made it to this farmer's spread, and he brought me here. Can't you see this uniform is too small?"

Corporal Warwick wrote on his report: *Denies all charges.* "Find the blacksmith," he said to Amos Tillit. "Tell 'im we need another ball and chain."

"How's about me bounty?"

"See the sergeant major in the mornin'."

Amos Tillet left for the blacksmith's shop. Stone turned to Corporal Warwick. "You follow up what I told you, you'll find out I'm telling the truth. I'm not a soldier."

"You're wearin' an Army uniform, you're a deserter. Any complaints, tell Sergeant Buford. One wrong move, you're a dead son of a bitch. Get my drift?"

"You're making a mistake. I'm an old friend of General Custer's."

"And I'm the King of Araby." Corporal Warwick was a string bean in blue, with a yellow bandanna around his throat, long drooping mustaches. He filled out his report. Stone's arms were bound, the corporal's pistol lay on the desk beside his right hand. Stone wanted to dive out the window, but he'd never make it. He'd straighten everything out in the morning when he talked to the guardhouse sergeant.

"Get goin'," Corporal Warwick said, aiming his revolver at Stone.

Stone left the guardhouse, heard soldiers singing to the music of a banjo in the distance. Lights flickered around the small Army post. Women in long dresses could be seen in the officers' area. Stone was tempted to call Fannies name, but the corporal might shoot him. The blacksmith occupied a shack near the guardhouse, the forge going full blast when Stone and Corporal Warwick entered. The blacksmith had huge rounded shoulders, wore a leather apron and no shirt, his hairy body covered with soot and sweat.

"Sit down and put yer leg on this here anvil," the blacksmith said.

Stone hesitated, Corporal Warwick aimed his gun at him. "I'm not a-goin' to tell you again."

Stone sat on the wooden chair, placed his leg on the anvil.

The blacksmith clasped an iron cuff around his ankle, caught the rivet in the end of the tongs, plunged it into tongues of flames. Light and shadow danced on the blacksmith's thick-bearded face. "What fort you run from?" he asked.

"I told you—I'm a civilian."

"And I'm General Custer."

"You tell General Custer that John Stone is here, I'll give you ten dollars."

The blacksmith looked at Corporal Warwick, they both burst into laughter. "Son of a bitch is crazy on top of everything else," the blacksmith said. "You sure you're not General Sheridan, or maybe Prince Albert?"

Stone pinched his lips together. The blacksmith pulled the white-hot rivet out of the flames, inserted it into the shackle, hairs singed on Stone's leg as the blacksmith raised his big steel hammer. Stone closed his eyes, the hammer whistled through the air and slammed the rivet. The shock wave jolted Stone's body; he felt an instant of sharp pain in his spine. When he opened his eyes, the cuff encircled his ankle.

"Next" said the blacksmith, thrusting another rivet into the fire.

Stone switched ankles. The blacksmith hammered another white-hot rivet, Stone's bones were jarred once more. Anger and fear welled up inside him. "You can't do this to me—goddamn bastards!"

Corporal Warwick slammed Stone's head with the stock of his rifle; Stone fell comatose to the floor. Corporal Warwick and the blacksmith dragged him back to the anvil, draped his wrists over it.

"Sounds like he's tellin' the truth," the blacksmith said. "That sure ain't his uniform he's a-wearin'."

"We go by the book," Corporal Warwick said. "Says throw the deserter in the guardhouse and report to the sergeant. Let him worry about it."

"Poor son of a bitch," replied the blacksmith, thrusting another rivet into the forge. "Sure hate to be in his shoes in the mornin' when Buford shows up fer duty. Buford hates deserters more'n anything else in the world."

3

STONE OPENED HIS eyes. Pitch-black, painful throb at the back of his head. He moved, felt heaviness at his wrists and ankles, heard shackles and chains. It all came back to him, guardhouse at Fort Hays, charged with desertion.

Tiny splinters of light entered cracks in the shutters. Stone vaguely made out sleeping forms on the floor. Something big and round rested near his right ankle. He touched the iron ball, moved it, estimated its weight at thirty-five pounds.

His eyes grew accustomed to the darkness. The slop bucket sat at one end of the room, emanating a horrendous odor entrapped by the closed shutters. The floor was bare ground and dirty straw. An old moth-eaten Army blanket lay beside Stone.

Tomorrow morning he'd straighten everything out. America was a nation of law. You needed a warrant to lock up a man. He reclined on the floor, pulling the smelly blanket over him. Lice that lived in the fabric crawled over him; he scratched absentmindedly as he closed his eyes. Exhausted, not fully recovered from pneumonia, he sank into deep slumber.

The guardhouse filled with snores and sighs, men slept all around him. Against the far wall, two heads bobbed up, Weaver and Ritterman, charged with insubordination, fighting, drunk on duty, awaiting transportation to the prison at Fort Leavenworth.

They crept silently across the floor, headed for the newcomer. When they reached him, Weaver whacked him on the head with a rock. Then they searched his pockets. Ritterman pulled off

Stone's boots, put them on his own feet, good fit. He left his worn boots next to Stone.

Lice sucked Stone's blood, he was out cold, a red knot growing on his head. He tried to roll over, ball and chain held him back. He coughed, snuggled next to the chain. On the far side of the room, Weaver went to sleep, while Ritterman guarded him. They took turns during the night, together they'd survive.

Stone hacked deep in his throat, iron cuffs cutting into the flesh of his arms and wrists. In the orderly room, Corporal Warwick snoozed on the cot, illuminated by the yellow effulgence of the lamp. The moon shone on the brave little fort in the wilderness, while the sun passed through the underbelly of the earth.

In the depths of his nightmare, Stone heard the familiar bugle call: reveille. He opened his eyes, saw the shutters of the guardhouse being flung open.

"Everybody up!" roared a deep baritone voice. "Drop yer cocks and grab yer socks!"

Stone was dazed from sleep, scratched his chest, heard his shackles and chains. He had lice many times during the war, knew the old familiar feeling. He reached for his boots, saw the beat-up pair.

The last shutter opened. Four men with balls and chains shuffled about the floor; Stone looked at their boots, spotted the nice comfortable ones he'd bought in Sundust. He raised his eyes, saw square jaw and shock of brown hair. "Give me my boots back," Stone said, "or I'll take 'em back."

Ritterman motioned with his hand. "Come git 'em, you feel like dyin'."

The door to the guardhouse was thrown open, and in the entrance, backlit from the corridor, stood a solidly built man with a short thick black beard. "Where's the deserter?"

"You the barracks sergeant?" Stone asked. "Glad to see you, because there's been a mix-up. I'm a civilian, a deserter took my clothes and robbed me. He left his uniform, you can see it doesn't fit me."

Sergeant Buford looked him up and down through little eyes set close together. He had a hairlip partially concealed by his beard. "Take 'im to my office," he said to Private Klappenbach.

Stone was glad he'd finally found somebody reasonable to talk with. He picked up his ball and carried it into the corridor, following Private Klappenbach. They came to the orderly room, Stone moved toward a chair.

"Where you goin', deserter?" The private lashed out his leg and kicked Stone's hip. "Stand at attention in front of the sergeant's desk, you goddamned idiot!"

"I'm a civilian."

"I'm George Washington. You want a bullet in yer ass?"

Stone lay his ball on the floor, stood at attention beside it. Buford hooked his jaunty forage cap on a peg, sat behind the desk. Private Klappenbach returned to the cell block. Only a few strands of frizzled hair covered Buford's tanned pate as he bent over the report.

"Mind if I have a seat?" Stone asked.

Sergeant Buford raised his face and looked into his eyes. "Stand where you are, deserter. You'll get no special coddlin' here."

"I told you I'm not a deserter. My clothes were stolen by a deserter."

Sergeant Buford stared at him for a few moments, then stood and walked around his desk. "All deserters tell the same lies. You don't fool me one goddamn bit. Enlist, git a free ride West, then head for the gold fields. Think you're smart, but you ain't. Yer first mistake was desertin'. Yer second was gittin' caught. Now you belong to me, and you don't git no third mistake."

Stone said, "When this gets straightened out, I'm coming back here. I'll have a little talk with you that you'll never forget."

Buford cocked an eye. "Threatenin' me?"

"This guardhouse is a disgrace. The Inspector General would like to know about it, I bet."

"He a friend of yours too, like General Custer? I read Corporal Warwick's report, you're goddamned bonkers on top of everything else."

"You bring General Custer in here, I'll show you who's bonkers."

Sergeant Buford narrowed his eyes. "I don't like yer tone of voice, you son of a bitch!"

He whacked Stone in the face with his riding crop, opening a three-inch gash. Stone raised his hands to protect himself, but the ball and chain slowed him down. The knotted end of the riding crop nicked Stone's ear, splitting it open. On the backswing, the riding crop struck just above Stone's left eye.

"Guard!" shouted Sergeant Buford.

The door opened, Private Klappenbach rushed in, aiming his bayonet at Stone's belly.

"Deserter just tried to escape," Sergeant Buford said. "Throw 'im in the hole."

In the headquarters orderly room, Sergeant Major Gillespie looked at the morning report from the guardhouse. A deserter had been brought in during the night. Claimed to be a civilian named John Stone.

Sergeant Major Gillespie scratched his head. *John Stone.* Sounded familiar, couldn't quite place it. Men came and went, he worried about supplies, ammunition, uniforms, drunkenness on duty, widespread venereal disease, a desertion rate that ran thirty to fifty percent, all companies understrength, injuns massacring women and children, promotion slow, no place to go.

"Ten-hut!"

Sergeant Major Gillespie shot to his feet. The door to the orderly room opened, and General Custer entered, followed by his entourage. Custer pulled off his wide-brimmed black hat and came to a stop before Sergeant Major Gillespie. "Anything for me to sign, Sergeant Major."

"On yer desk, sir."

Sergeant Major Gillespie was tempted to tell General Custer about the prisoner who claimed to be a friend of his, but feared the general's volatile moods. Young admiring officers followed the war hero to his office. "At ease!" one of them shouted. Sergeant Major Gillespie returned to his desk, the name *John Stone* buried deep in the forgotten convolutions of his brain.

Bleeding from riding crop cuts, John Stone carried his iron ball to the muddy area behind the guardhouse. Horses had been kept here recently, urine and manure potent in the air. They came to a wooden hatch covered with a boulder. Two men lifted the boulder, Corporal Warwick kicked the hatch aside. Hole ten feet deep, six feet wide, with a pot and canteen at the bottom.

"Get in," the corporal said.

"I'm a civilian," Stone replied, "and once that's found out, I'll get out of here. When I do, I'll remember you."

"You just threatened a noncommissioned officer in the United States Army. Throw 'im down, boys."

Thc soldiers grabbed Stone's arms, he struggled to break loose, Corporal Warwick conked him with the butt of his rifle. They dragged him to edge of the hole, kicked him in, his ball and chain dragged him to the bottom. He landed with a crash and didn't open his eyes for a long time.

Slipchuck advanced toward Sergeant Major Gillespie's desk, hat in hand. "My friend John Stone check in yet?"

Sergeant Major Gillespie looked at the broken-down old man standing in front of him. "What was the name?"

"John Stone."

The name rang a dim bell, but Sergeant Major Gillespie had a hundred louder gongs going constantly in his head, reminding him to do something important, or not to do something critical. "Ain't you been in here before?"

"Every day."

Sergeant Major Gillespie wanted to bawl him out for the interruption, but the geezer was a civilian. A soldier could lose everything he'd built for thirty years because of civilians. They paid a few dollars in taxes and thought they owned the Army, the White House, and all the ships at sea.

Slipchuck walked out of the orderly room, into the sunshine. He unhitched Buckshot from the rail, climbed into the saddle, rode toward the front gate, worrying about John Stone, who lay sweating in the hole less than two hundred yards away.

General Custer entered his house, took off his buckskin jacket, hung it in the hall closet. His wife, Libbie Custer, descended the stairs, holding her skirt with one hand. "What's wrong?"

He gazed out the window at the endless prairie. "Damned place is getting me down. Same routine day after day. Wanted more for us than this."

She came behind him, wrapped her arms around his waist. "We'll get through somehow, as long as we have each other."

"Maybe we should get out of the Army. Can't spend the rest of our lives in this hellhole."

Dogs barked on their front porch, followed by a knock. General Custer and Libby separated. Eliza, their black maid, opened the door. It was Sergeant Major Gillespie standing at attention, hat beneath his arm. "Have to speak to the general," he said. "Emergency."

"What is it, Gillespie?" asked Custer.

"Major Scanlon ain't been seen for five days, sir. Some of the men think he might be dead. Maybe you should look in on him."

"You look in on him, Sergeant Major Gillespie. I have complete confidence in your judgment in these matters."

"You're the onliest man on this post what ranks Major Scanlon. It's a job for the commanding officer, sir."

General Custer's long mustaches twitched as he wondered what to do about his provost marshal. Libbie joined them near the door. "Did I hear the both of you talking about Major Scanlon? Well, he's on his way across the parade ground right now, and it doesn't appear as though he's going to make it."

General Custer and Sergeant Major Gillespie rushed to the nearest window. An officer staggered toward the guardhouse. His hat was askew on his head, sword too far forward on his belt, shirt mostly untucked. Soldiers clipping grass nearby laughed openly.

Sergeant Major Gillespie said, "There's also the matter of Lieutenant Classen, requires yer attention, General."

Custer's sunburned features shone like bronze in the light from the window. "What matter are you referring to?"

"Whether or not ladies should be present."

Lieutenant Classen, a West Point graduate only three months ago, had been attacked by injuns while on a patrol. He fled, but his first sergeant assumed command of the men and easily beat the injuns off. Cowardice in the face of the enemy. Tomorrow morning he was scheduled to be drummed out of the Seventh Cavalry. A decision had to be made about whether or not women would be permitted to attend the ceremony.

"I think," Libbie said, "the general needs more time to think it over."

Sergeant Major Gillespie replied, "Can't wait too long. Need to get the orders out." He threw a smart salute, performed a flawless about-face, marched out of the Custer residence.

The moment the door closed, Libby said, "Poor Lieutenant Classen has been humiliated enough. You needn't make it worse by letting women see his shame."

"You don't want to attend the ceremony, that's your decision. I won't tell the women on this post how to lead their lives."

"You know very well most will go to the ceremony, out of morbid curiosity. Not every man can be brave. It's not Lieutenant Classen's fault. He's such a sensitive boy."

"He's a man, not a boy. When I was his age . . ."

"You were on General McClellan's staff," she interrupted, "and you'd already won your first citation for bravery. But everyone can't be like you. Lieutenant Classen doesn't belong in the Army. It's enough that he has to be humiliated before the garrison, but not the women too. Something like that could destroy him. If he committed suicide, how would you feel?"

He looked at her in the bright afternoon sunlight streaming through the window. They'd grown up childhood sweethearts in Monroe, Michigan; she the judge's daughter, he the son of a poor farmer whose copperhead political views were unpopular. She'd been high above him in social rank, yet he'd won her, and now wanted to win her again. He moved toward her, placed his knobby weather-reddened hands on her waist.

"Don't forget," she said, "you have to give Sergeant Major Gillespie your decision."

"Already made," he murmured, brushing his lips against her ear. "No women at the drumming out."

"I think my general deserves a reward for his compassion. What do you think he might appreciate?"

With a sweep of his powerful arm, General Custer carried her to the stairs.

Stone lay semiconscious in the bottom of the hole, flies buzzing around his head, stench and heat unbearable. His throat was the dry bark of a tree, his stomach cramped, body drenched with sweat. Not enough room to lie down and stretch out. *Every time I turn around, I get into trouble.* The planked trapdoor above him moved. Bright sunlight drove a spike through his brain. He closed his eyes and cringed like a rat exposed to the light of day.

"Time fer dinner," said a voice above him.

A bucket containing a canteen and bowl of something was lowered to him. Stone fumbled for the canteen, unscrewed the lid unsteadily, drank lukewarm alkaline water. The trapdoor was replaced, dirt and pebbles fell onto John Stone, darkness descended once more. He groped for the bowl of soup, raised it to his nose, smelled like dishwater. He lifted the spoon and tasted some. Probably *was* dishwater. Starved, he drank it anyway. He could barely breathe, the stench from the slop bucket overpowering, germs of pneumonia coursed through his bloodstream. His eyes rolled into his head and he went slack in the bottom of the hole, breath coming in short gasps.

Private Klappenbach rushed into the guardhouse orderly room. "Think that son of a bitch in the hole is 'bout ready to give up the ghost."

Sergeant Buford glanced at something behind Private Klappenbach. Klappenbach turned and was shocked to see Major Scanlon seated on a chair, uniform rumpled, eyes bloodshot, half closed.

"What's this about the hole?" he asked in a gravelly voice.

"Deserter," Sergeant Buford said. "Threatened me and Private Klappenbach."

"A man dies in that hole, we can all be court-martialed. Get him the hell out of there!"

Sergeant Buford winked. "He kicks the bucket, who'll know? Fill the hole over his head and dig another one."

Major Scanlon pushed himself unsteadily to his feet. He'd shaved and trimmed his graying mustache that morning, but his hand had slipped, the mustache was lopsided. He appeared ludicrious, the parody of an officer. He teetered from side to side as he declared, "You'll not kill a prisoner in this guardhouse without full judicial review! Bring that man to me this instant!"

Sergeant Buford drew himself to his full height behind the desk. "Sir, the prisoner tried to kill me. General Custer himself authorized the hole."

"I said bring that prisoner in here!"

"You're undercuttin' the discipline in this here guardhouse, Major Scanlon!"

"You'd better do what I say, Sergeant Buford, or I'll rip those stripes off your damned sleeve!"

Sergeant Buford gazed at Major Scanlon calmly, wondering if he should shoot him. The major was drunk and erratic, had to be shot before he killed someone by mistake. Sergeant Buford weighed the possibilities. Too many people around. He turned to Klappenbach. "Bring the deserter here."

Klappenbach left the orderly room, Major Scanlon took an unsteady step toward Sergeant Buford, they were alone. "You're the scum of the earth, Buford," Major Scanlon said, lowering his hand to his gun. "I know all about you and the way you treat the prisoners in this guardhouse. You're sick in your goddamn mind, like a lot of other people on the post I could name. One of these days you'll go too far, you'll be the one in the guardhouse, mark my words."

Sergeant Buford stared him in the eye. "You mark mine. I'm goin' to kill you. You couldn't even handle yer own woman. All the officers was a-plunkin' her, and you didn't know nawthin' about it, or didn't want to know." Sergeant Buford's hand hovered above his regulation Colt revolver. "We could hear her callin' you *idiot* all the way to the guardhouse. You was old enough to be her daddy. You know what I think you are, Major Scanlon? I think you're just a dirty old man."

Major Scanlon went for his gun, so did Sergeant Buford. The door opened, Private Klappenbach and Private Delancy carried the prisoner into the orderly room. Stone was out cold, head lolling lifelessly to the side, mouth hanging open. The prisoner had been beaten, his uniform didn't fit, white as a sheet.

"He's not a deserter from this post," Major Scanlon said.

"Prob'ly Fort Dodge," Sergeant Buford replied.

"What did he say when you charged him."

"Said he weren't no deserter."

Commonest alibi of all, Major Scanlon reflected. They'd send his description to posts in the department, a few would ask for him, he'd make the rounds, if nobody could identify him he'd be set free. Could take a year or more. The slow grinding process of justice in the frontier army.

Klappenbach and Delancy carried Stone to the cell block, the door closed behind them.

Major Scanlon slurred, "We should settle this disagreement off post, on our own time."

"Tell me where and when, sir. I'll be there."

"How about tomorrow at midnight, the Wakhatchie River crossing?"

"I can see horns growin' out of yer head, that woman cheated on you so much, you damned fool."

"My gun will respond to that remark, and your other insults, tomorrow night at the Wakhatchie River crossing."

"Wouldn't miss it for the world."

Major Scanlon walked toward the door, regulation spurs jangling, yellow stripes on his pants crooked, shirt half unbuttoned. Sergeant Buford gazed at him with contempt. Scanlon was a hero of the Civil War, but Buford served in that conflict too, and knew for a fact that many inflated reputations came out of it; Scanlon was probably just another of them. You son of a bitch, you go to that Wakhatchie crossing, it be the last place you see.

Stone felt something cool and wet against his lips. He opened his eyes, saw a tin cup full of water, somebody was raising his head, he sipped the water, dank and foul, but it moistened his mouth.

"How you feel?" asked a voice.

Stone looked up, saw tiny teeth, shifty furtive manner.

"Kind of weak," Stone replied.

"What's your name?"

"John Stone."

"I'm Anthony Antonelli. What fort you run from?"

"I'm not Army . . . but nobody believes me."

"I'm a civilian too, or leastways I was a few months ago. Should never've joined up. Biggest mistake of my life." He glanced around suspiciously. "They wake you in the middle of the night to fight injuns, and when you're not doin' that, it's pig work 'round the fort. All I did was spit in Captain Benteen's face. We'll go to Fort Leavenworth for a few years. They can't kill men like us."

"I'm not a deserter," Stone replied. "They'll never put me in Fort Leavenworth."

The water revived him, a louse crawled into his left armpit, he scratched. Against the far wall sat Weaver and Ritterman, and Stone looked at his boots on Ritterman's feet. Stone tried to get up, but his muscles weren't functioning properly.

"When you're stronger," Antonelli said, "you'll get him. I'll watch your back. We stick together, we'll get through all right."

"Is there a way I can get a message to General Custer? He and I are old friends."

Antonelli looked at him sadly. "You poor son of a bitch, they broke your mind."

"Is there somebody we can bribe to carry a message to Custer?"

"Bribe with what?"

Stone narrowed his eyes in suspicion. "How do you know I have no money?"

Antonelli shrugged. "Them two buzzards went through your pockets pretty good. Maybe you can see General Custer at the drumming out in the mornin'."

Stone gazed at Antonelli with new interest. "You been on this post long?"

" 'Bout a month."

"You must know who Marie Scanlon is."

"Woman caused more trouble on this post than a hive of bees."

"What's she done?"

"All the ladies was a-fightin' with her, but she's gone now."

"Where to?"

"Didn't stop at the guardhouse to say good-bye. What's she to you?"

"Friend of mine." Stone reached for the picture of Marie he usually carried in his shirt pocket, it had disappeared. He gazed across the room at Weaver and Ritterman. "When'd she leave?"

"About a week ago."

"What about her husband?"

"Ain't been sober since."

"She go alone?"

"Left with a gambler."

"Get his name?"

Antonelli shook his head. Stone rose wobbly to his feet, held the bars of a small window, looked at the prairie. What the hell happened? Madness welled up, he reared back his fist, heaved a punch at the wall, but held back an inch before impact. Calm down. Get out of the guardhouse, find out where she went. He felt sick and demoralized, and his feet hurt. He glanced across the cell at Ritterman.

"Come git 'em." Ritterman reached into his pocket, pulled out a blade. "I'll carve you like the Christmas turkey."

Stone felt a wave of dizziness. His head cleared, rush of wind through his ears. He still wasn't recovered, needed a good hot meal. Then maybe he could do something.

Something rustled next to him, Antonelli holding something in his hand. "Take it."

Stone reached down, a knife with a three-inch blade made from a spoon dropped into his hand. He slipped the knife into his boot. "When do we eat?"

"They'll bring the slops soon, but I don't know if you can eat it. Takes practice to beat the smell."

General Custer walked past officers' row, slapping his riding crop against his leg. Always something to worry about. His men were the dregs of seven continents. They called him Iron Butt, General Custard, and a lot of other unflattering epithets, while the Michigan Wolverines had idolized him, would follow him anywhere, even copied his eccentric uniforms.

Penpushers and hacks in Washington exiled him to the middle of nowhere, where he'd be forgotten. Libbie was restless, he couldn't blame her. A million ridiculous details bedeviled him. Everywhere he turned, something required his attention.

He approached Major Scanlon's house, the front door slighty ajar. General Custer's hunting dogs yipped and danced behind him. One poked the door with his nose, it creaked wider.

General Custer pushed the door wide open, debris everywhere. A dark form lay on the sofa. The stench of whiskey and vomit lay heavy in the air, broken glass crunched beneath General Custer's boots.

The figure on the sofa stirred. Stained and wrinkled uniform, buttons undone, belt loosened, Major Scanlon drunk again. He struggled to reach his feet, threw a sloppy salute.

" . . . reporting for duty . . . sir."

General Custer returned the salute. "Have a seat, Scanlon. We've got to talk."

Major Scanlon remained at attention. "Sir, before you say . . . anything . . . I take full responsibility for . . . for . . ." He wondered what he'd done wrong, besides being drunk. His alcohol-drenched mind gave him a dim image of the guardhouse. Had he done something wrong in the guardhouse? He honestly didn't know, and stood befuddled, eyes at half mast, shirt blotched with his last meal.

"I said, have a seat."

Major Scanlon dropped to the sofa. Custer saw chicken bones on the floor, broken bottles, and furniture. The provost marshal had busted his home apart after learning his wife had left him.

"Major Scanlon, can you hear me?"

"Perfectly clear, sir."

"I can't keep covering for you. You've got to get the hell out of here. I don't care if you resign, fly to the moon, whatever, but you've got one week to do it, or I'll have to apply the Articles of War. We can have no more spectacles such as you presented this afternoon on the parade ground. You're confined to quarters until further notice. You've got to pull yourself together."

It was silent a few moments, then Major Scanlon dropped his face into his hands. "She . . . left me," he said in a faint whisper, as though he couldn't believe it.

"Don't throw your career away. One of these days we'll go to war against the injuns, and I'll need good officers behind me. Don't let me down. We've been through too much together."

Major Scanlon's head hung low. "Can't live . . . without her." His body was wracked with sobs.

General Custer scrutinized him carefully. Hard to believe this rough cavalry officer could be hurt so deeply. He cried like a hurt little boy. General Custer placed his hand on Major Scanlon's shoulder. "You're an old Regular Army man, you came up from the ranks. Don't make me do something that might cause both of us pain. It's never bad as you think. If you came through the war, you can get through this." General Custer shook Major Scanlon's shoulder. "You're an officer."

Major Scanlon heard General Custer and his dogs receding into the distance. He gazed at the rubble of the home he'd shared with his wife. The emptiness in his heart was unbearable. Friends warned him not to marry her, too many years separated them, she was moody and wild, threatened to leave many times, finally did, now he was alone, part of him dead and the rest in torment. The foul taste grew strong in his mouth. He reached for the bottle of whiskey, to wash it away.

Someone touched Stone's shoulder. He opened his eyes. Antonelli's face was suspended above him. "It's time."

Stone raised his head. On the other side of the cell, in the dimness, Ritterman rose to his feet, shaking dirt and straw from his clothes. Cool and dark in the guardhouse, a few slim rays of light entered through cracks in the shutters.

Ritterman held his knife in his right hand, the blade gleamed as he advanced toward Stone, blanket wrapped around his left hand, wrist, and forearm. Stone got to his feet, cramped and pinched in Ritterman's boots. He pulled out the knife with the three-inch blade, not nearly as good as his old Apache knife, but it'd have to do.

Antonelli handed him the blanket. "Go for his belly."

The boots impeded Stone's movement, he'd be better off in his bare feet. He sat again, pulled off the boots, cold floor against the soles of his feet. Ritterman pulled out the picture of Marie. "This a real silver frame?" he asked.

"You won't have it long," Stone replied.

Ritterman snored derisively. "I'm a-gonna carve you a new asshole."

Stone rolled his shoulders, loosened up. His heartbeat was a steady tom-tom, he felt eighty percent of normal, had to get his boots back, and the picture of Marie.

"Who is she?" Ritterman asked, holding the picture up to a ray of light. "Looks like Major Scanlon's former wife, biggest whore in Kansas." Ritterman laughed, rubbed the picture against his pants.

Stone's blood curdled in his veins. Ritterman placed the picture of Marie in his back pocket. "I like to see a man's face when I stick the knife in."

Stone's legs didn't have their usual spring. *Can't try anything fancy, hunker down and go for his gut.* Antonelli walked beside Stone, stiff as a board, arms straight down his side, knife in his hand pointing at the ground. His pose reminded Stone of a fighting cock's strut.

Weaver accompanied Ritterman to the center of the guardhouse floor, chains clanging in the darkness. Other prisoners watched from the sidelines. Stone looked into Ritterman's eyes, saw two cold blue chips of ice, no human warmth in those diabolical orbs.

"Want these boots?" Ritterman asked Stone, flashing his knife through the air. "You know what you got to do."

Antonelli and Weaver stepped to the side, eyes never leaving each other. The main event was Stone and Ritterman, facing each other in the middle of the floor. Ritterman was four inches shorter than Stone, sturdily built, dressed in his blue Army uniform, knife blade up in his fist.

"Never did like deserters," Ritterman said. "Deserters are lower'n skunks, in my book."

Stone went into his knife-fighter's crouch, and circled to the left, dragging his ball and chain. Ritterman got low. Stone was flatfooted, inching closer, both men hampered by shackles.

"I had a sister like Marie Scanlon," Ritterman said, a goad in his voice, "I'd plug her hole with a cork, but she'd think of some other way, a whore like that."

Stone wanted to skin and bone him alive, but forced himself to concentrate on the basics. He glanced at his boots on Ritterman's feet. A man can't survive without good boots. The iron cuff chafed his leg as he came to a stop in front of Ritterman. They bobbed and weaved, searching for angles through which to push their blades.

Raised in the back alleys of Milwaukee, Ritterman believed in the all-out aggressive charge, especially effective against an opponent with poor maneuverability. Growling like a longhorn bull, he lowered his head and pushed the blanket toward Stone's face, while jabbing the knife in his other hand toward Stone's midsection.

Stone ducked underneath Ritterman's blanket, slammed his own blanket into Ritterman's knife. Ritterman was wide open for a split second, Stone drove his blade toward Ritterman's belly. Ritterman shrieked as Stone pushed the knife in all the way, ripped to the side. Ritterman's guts spilled out like a nest of angry rattlesnakes.

Ritterman fell at Stone's feet, gurgling in his throat. One jugular thrust from Stone's knife put an end to the death rattle. Ritterman lay still on the floor. Antonelli and Weaver faced each other tensely, a nervous tremor on Weaver's face, while Antonelli was braced and poised.

Stone dropped to his knees, pulled the boots off Ritterman's feet. A foul stench filled the guardhouse. Stone donned the boots. Weaver stepped backward, lowered his knife. Antonelli watched him carefully through slitted eyes. Weaver retreated to the shadows, the fight gone out of him. Stone rolled Ritterman and pulled Marie's picture from his back pocket. Marie was streaked with blood, Stone wiped it off on Ritterman's pants. He arose, dragged his ball and chain to the far wall.

"You and me ought to team up, bust out of here," Antonelli said. "All we need is a gun."

"Don't need a gun," Stone said. "General Custer is an old friend of mine."

Antonelli grinned, showing tiny pointed teeth. "Sure, and then you'll walk on water like Jesus Christ, right?"

Stone inserted the makeshift knife into his boot. After he got out of the guardhouse, Sergeant Buford would be next on his list. The iron cuffs cut into his skin, inflaming fresh sores, as he tried to make himself comfortable on the cold dank floor.

Slipchuck sat in a corner of the Tumbleweed Saloon, drinking whiskey. A substantial portion of his wages was gone. Time to be prudent. No more whores unless bargain rates were offered. Watch the passing show and stay out of trouble.

A portly man in his fifties, wearing a dude suit and a derby, strode out of the thick cigarette and cigar smoke. "I was talking to a soldier at the bar, and he said you're Ray Slipchuck, zat so?"

Slipchuck looked him over, no gun showing, probably a derringer in his frock-coat pocket. "What of it?"

"You the same Ray Slipchuck who shot Frank Quarternight in Sundust a few days back?" The man sat down, heavy jowls shaking like jelly covered with sideburns. "Heard it was an elderly gentleman, such as yerself, beard and all. Don't worry, I won't say nothin'."

"Don't know what you're talkin' about," Slipchuck said, turning away, but it was true. He'd killed the famous Texas gunfighter with a lucky shot in a bizarre showdown.

"Buy you a drink?" the man asked.

"Don't mind if I do."

"Waitress—a bottle of whiskey if you please!"

Slipchuck appraised his benefactor, just the kind of man he wished he was, fancy duds, plenty of coins, all the women he wants. The gambler pulled the cork and filled Slipchuck's glass to the rim. "My name's Daugherty. Drink up."

Daugherty pulled out a gold cigar case. Slipchuck's eyes widened at the sight of stogies laid out like evil dark turds. He selected one, bit off the end, spit it at the cuspidor, missed, another gob of gunk on a floor covered with whiskey stains, cigarette butts, an old sock, half a man's shirt, dabs of dried blood left over from the last brawl, a few steak bones.

Slipchuck hollowed his gray-bearded cheeks, sucked in the mellow smoke, his head disappeared in a blue cloud. Aged in brandy casks, the stogies were the best money could buy. Slipchuck leaned back in his chair, glass of whiskey in his other hand. "You know the gambler what ran off with that officer's wife a while back?"

"Derek Canfield was a friend of mine."

"What was he like?"

"Smooth line of shit. He somethin' to you?"

"My pard knew the Scanlon woman."

"That was one pretty filly. Sashayed around this town like she owned it. Didn't care what anybody thought when she shacked with Canfield at the hotel. Never turn your back on that woman, that's my advice to you. I'm a ramblin' gamblin' man, never claimed to be nothin' else, and when I make a bet, it ain't no idle notion. I'll give you three to one odds she's dead within a year."

Light flickered in the windows of the sutler's store as General Custer passed. Guttural laughter emanated from the squat ramshackle building, someone plunked a guitar. If Custer had his way, he'd tear the stinkhouse down, but the men wouldn't stand for it. Custer didn't need a full-scale rebellion on his service record. You could only push men so far.

He passed the sutler's store, boots crunching gravel, hunting dogs leaping and tossing around him, serenading the fort with their choruses of yelps and barks, probably keeping somebody awake, but Custer loved them. A man would betray you, never your dogs.

General Custer entered the bachelor officers' quarters, a row of small square one-story cabins. Lights were extinguished in all except one. General Custer rapped his bony knuckles against the door as his dogs did back turns and wild swirls, snapping their teeth.

The door was opened by Lieutenant Classen, on the chubby side, thinning brown hair, serious.

"May I come in?" General Custer asked.

Lieutenant Classen stepped to the side. General Custer entered a small room with a watercolor of a gray-haired matron on the wall. He angled his head so he could read the spine of the book on the desk:

POETICAL WORKS
by
Samuel Taylor Coleridge

A glass of brandy stood beside the book. "Hope you're not drinking too much of that," Custer said. "Do you have a loaded weapon in this place?"

"I won't shoot myself, if that's what you're worried about, sir."

General Custer looked him in the eye. The last thing he needed on his record was the suicide of a junior officer. "You're sure of that?"

"You have my word, sir. But perhaps you might not accept the word of a coward."

"Some men aren't cut out for Army life," Custer said. "I had to throw the book at you, but don't take it personally. You ever need a recommendation from me, just ask. Who knows, maybe you're the lucky one. The rest of us're stuck at Fort Hays, and you'll go back East with your whole future in front of you." General Custer extended his hand. "Good luck to you."

Lieutenant Classen shook the proffered hand. *A cool customer,* General Custer thought. *Never know what's going on behind that expressionless face.* He expected Lieutenant Classen to thank him for the visit, it wasn't every day General Custer dropped in on junior officers. "If you don't mind, Lieutenant, I'd sleep easier if I had your service revolver."

Lieutenant Classen opened a drawer, pulled out the gun, pointed it at Custer. For a terrifying moment, the Boy General thought he'd be assassinated.

Lieutenant Classen turned the revolver around and passed it butt end first to General Custer. "Want my sword too?"

"We'll get it in the morning. Just stand steady when they start the drums. You have friends coming to meet you, I understand?"

General Custer walked toward the sutler's store, riding crop slapping his leg, brow creased in thought. Classen would be ruined for life, a man can't run from something like a drum-out. Wherever he went, the taint would follow. He'd enter his club, they'd snub him. A man without a country.

General Custer had known fear. Every man had his breaking

point. Better shot through the head in a cavalry charge than rot with age.

He came to the sutler's store, climbed the stairs. A voice hollered: "Ten-*hut!*" Scramble of chairs and tables, General Custer opened the door. Soldiers and officers stood stiffly at attention, uniforms disheveled, struggling to maintain balance. General Custer saw the officer he wanted standing in the corner next to a table with a bottle, glass, ashtray, and cigar sending up a trail of smoke.

"As you were," Custer said casually, walking toward the officer. The other men drank up quickly, rushed to get out of there. The captain at the table looked at General Custer disdainfully as he approached. The captain had large bulging eyes and prematurely white hair furling beneath his campaign hat.

"Want to have a word with you, Benteen. Have a seat and listen."

Both men lowered to chairs. Captain Benteen wore his hat tilted low over his eyes; General Custer's black brim was pulled down also. General Custer pushed the bottle out of the way. He and Benteen took an instant dislike to each other when they met nearly four years ago. Their relations had worsened ever since.

"At the drum-out tomorrow," General Custer said, "I don't want you to go too hard on Lieutenant Classen. Just get it over with."

"You're awful easy on Classen, General. Can't help wondering why. The scared little puppy should be shot at dawn, and if you're looking for someone to pull the trigger, I volunteer here and now. Maybe you're sympathetic to cowards because you're one yourself."

General Custer brought himself under control. They stared into each other's eyes, both unwilling to face the inevitable court-martial for shooting a fellow officer in public. A few seconds passed. General Custer felt in command of the situation once more.

"You've received your orders," he said levelly to Benteen. "Do you have any questions?"

"Why'd you leave Major Elliot behind?"

General Custer thought he'd lose control, but focused his iron will and clamped down. He didn't need a life sentence at Fort Leavenworth for gunning down Benteen.

At the Battle of the Washita, Major Elliot and his detachment became lost, cut off, and massacred by injuns. Custer had been blamed for the disaster. If you're deep in hostile territory, you can't sacrifice a regiment for a hand who went astray, and Custer had had every reason to believe Major Elliot returned to safety. The Boy General was a fighting field commander, and would match his war record against anybody's. Benteen's a jealous drunken complainer, not worth anybody's time.

General Custer walked toward the door. Captain Benteen felt like shooting him in the back, but didn't want Fort Leavenworth either. General Custer left the sutler's store, Benteen returned to his chair. Major Elliot had been a friend, while General Custer was a blowhard and liar. Everybody loved old Iron Butt except the men who served under him.

General Custer walked home, unsettled by his encounter with Benteen. The Army was rife with incompetent officers who undermined every enterprise with their pointless nit-picking questions to show how smart they were.

In the old days with the Wolverines, when he hollered *forward,* they advanced. They never questioned his authority, never dragged their feet. The Seventh Cavalry needed a major victory to bring them together behind his banner, but Washington couldn't agree on an injun policy, and the Seventh Cavalry languished on the plains.

Something slipped from an alley straight ahead, General Custer ducked into the shadows, pulled his service revolver. Could be an injun. How'd he get through the pickets? The man came closer, moonlight flashed on his face: Lieutenant Forrest. General Custer stepped into the open. Lieutenant Forrest went for his gun.

"As you were," said General Custer.

Lieutenant Forrest's mouth hung open in surprise, he snapped to attention. "Evening, sir."

General Custer wrinkled his nose. Ladies' perfume clung to the young officer, they found him irresistible, his affair with Major Scanlon's wife had scandalized the post. "Out for a walk, Mr. Forrest?" He tried to remember which of his officers' wives wore the fragrance. It had a familiar rose scent. At the next dance, he'd sniff the wench out. "I have a new assignment for you. I'm appointing you new acting provost marshal, effective right now. Tell Sergeant Major Gillespie to have the order on my desk first thing in the morning."

Lieutenant Forrest shuffled his feet nervously. "I'm sorry about what happened with Major Scanlon, sir. I caused you concern, couldn't help myself. Marie Scanlon was quite a . . . well, quite a woman."

General Custer wondered if he could say no to a woman like Marie Scanlon. "Try to be more discreet in the future, Mr. Forrest. We wouldn't want an irate husband to shoot you."

They saluted. A dog chewed on Lieutenant Forrest's heel. Custer walked home exhausted. The peacetime Army took more out of him than hard combat without sleep for days.

He entered his home, climbed the stairs, found Libbie in bed, her lovely tresses adorning the pillow, reading her journal entries, chewing the end of the pen like a schoolgirl. "What happened to you?" she asked.

Custer looked at the open window. Not Libbie and Lieutenant Forrest. The shavetail wouldn't dare. Still, he had to know. Summoning his famous courage, he leaned forward, sniffed Libbie's perfume, afraid of what might strike his nose.

Lemon scent, unlike the rosebushes emanating from Lieutenant Forrest. General Custer breathed a sigh of grateful relief as he nuzzled his nose into his wife's throat.

"Did you speak with Lieutenant Classen?" she asked. "How's he holding up?"

"Hard to say, because he barely spoke. I took his service revolver just in case. Then I ran into Captain Benteen. Of all the regiments in the Army, they had to send that bellyaching troublemaking imbecile to me. He'll be the death of me yet."

Stone was awakened by an itch in a sensitive spot. He scratched, gnashed his teeth, lice driving him mad, couldn't get a good night's sleep. He saw the body of Ritterman lying on the floor. Should be quite a show when the corpse was found in the morning.

Stone shuffled his ball and chain to the water bucket, dipped in, drank water with something threadlike and crackling, an insect down the hatch. On the way to his blanket, he passed the window, yearned to see the sky. He leaned against the shutter, peeked through a crack, saw the parade field and bare flagpole, halyards banging in the wind.

He'd come so far, Marie was gone, he was locked up. Would his bad luck ever change? A coyote wailed mournfully in the distance, and Stone was tempted to open his mouth and reply. He crawled beneath his blanket, scratched. In his dream, the lobo sat alone on a cliff, snout raised high, serenading the moon.

4

IT WAS MORNING, and Tomahawk cropped grass on a vast plain. He was nervous and frightened, but remained in the vicinity of the fort in case John Stone came by.

He glanced suddenly behind him. A wildcat or injun could attack out of nowhere. He chewed the frothy dew-laden grass. Winter was coming. Got to move south before snow. He didn't want to leave John Stone, but had to be sensible.

He heard something. In the distance, a lone horse trotted toward him. His first reaction was run like hell, but no rider sat on the horse's back. Tomahawk waited curiously to see what the other horse would do.

The strawberry roan mare came closer. She twitched her tail, showed rippling flanks, bent down, chewed grass. Tomahawk stared at her in awe. She was one of the wild ones.

Come with me. We are going to the land of the sun.

Sergeant Buford unlocked the door to the guardhouse, Private Klappenbach carried a big black pot full of thick gruel with bones, bits of meat and fat. It smelled ghastly, but Stone was starved. He and the other prisoners shuffled their shackles and chains toward it, holding wooden bowls.

Sergeant Buford looked past them to a dark form on the floor. "What's that!" He entered the cell, slapping his riding crop against his leg in imitation of his idol, General George Armstrong Custer.

"I'll be a son of a bitch." He rolled Ritterman's stiffening corpse over. "Who did it!"

Nobody said a word. Sergeant Buford rushed to the head of the line, where Antonelli stood with his bowl. He flipped his riding crop, a cut appeared on Antonelli's nose.

"Fall in!" Sergeant Buford hollered. "Right here—right now—no food till we git to the bottom of this!"

Antonelli and the other prisoners lined up. Stone advanced to the stew pot and filled his bowl with the dense oleaginous substance. Sergeant Buford stared at him for a few moments in astonishment. "I gave you a goddamn *command!* You got shit in yer ears?"

"I'm not in your Army."

"Don't talk back to me!" Sergeant Buford raised his arm to whack Stone across the face with his riding crop, but Stone caught his wrist in midair.

"Wouldn't do it if I were you."

Private Delancy and Pfc. Klappenbach dived on Stone from behind, holding his shoulders. Stone bucked like a mustang, and flung them through the air. Corporal Warwick smashed Stone in the head with the butt of his rifle. Stone dropped to the floor like a sack of flour.

Sergeant Buford noticed something strange. Stone wore the same boots Ritterman had on earlier in the day. A fight over leather, looked like. "This time you done it, deserter," Sergeant Buford said to Stone's motionless body. "You'll git the firing squad, 'fore I'm finished with you." He turned to Corporal Warwick. "Drop him in the hole."

"What hole?" Lieutenant Forrest entered the guardhouse, campaign hat slanted rakishly over his eyes, silver bars gleaming on his gold shoulder boards. "What's going on here, Buford?"

"This man attacked me, sir."

Lieutenant Forrest looked at the unconscious trooper on the floor. "Who is he?"

"Deserter. He killed that man over there."

Lieutenant Forrest noticed the unconscious prisoner. "You see him do it?"

"No, but he's wearin' the other one's boots, sir."

"You'll need more proof than that to throw a man in the hole. Two sides to every story, and we don't have time for a courtroom debate. Give the prisoners their breakfast, then take them to the formation."

Lieutenant Forrest walked out of the guardhouse. Sergeant Buford waited until his footsteps could no longer be heard, then turned to the other prisoners. "Any of you girls see 'im kill Ritterman? Come on, don't be shy." He gazed into each of their faces, one after the other, but no one said anything. "So that's the way it is, eh? All right—you asked for it—as of right now you're on half rations, and I'll see if I can find some nice work for you around the post, like carrying boulders on yer shoulders *till you drop in yer stinkin' tracks*!"

Sergeant Major Gillespie stood in front of the mirror, scraped the straight razor across his cheek. Fifty years old, but solid as a man of thirty, he examined himself in the mirror. "Damn!" A trickle of blood appeared in the cleft between his chin.

Marsha Gillespie, his wife, entered the kitchen. "One of these days you'll cut yer head off," she declared. "A body would think you'd know how to use one of them things by now."

He held the shiny implement in the air and bared his teeth. "This is a razor," he explained, "and it's sharp. You could cut a man's head off with it. Anybody who shaves nicks himself once in a while. It's the nature of the beast. Back in the days when I was single, I wore a beard, didn't have to go through this goddamned torture every morning."

"You don't like it, go back to the barracks where you come from. You'll be a private again inside a month."

Sergeant Major Gillespie who had been up and down the ranks many times knew she was right. The barracks were crowded with lonely men who drank too much. Inevitable disagreements produced constant brawling, and the only thing to do was get in the middle of it. Then he met the sergeant major's daughter, married her, now was a sergeant major himself. Every trooper at Fort Hays trembled in his presence, but she treated him like a dumb recruit. He'd passed from one condition of subservience to another, and sometimes longed for all-night poker games at payday stakes, parties at the hog pens, saloons, the camaraderie of the barracks.

She placed a mug of coffee on the table next to him, the fragrance of Brazil rose to his nostrils. He raised the coffee to his lips, sipped the strong hot beverage. She'd subjugated him with good food, drink, and her truly magnificent bosom, the feature that caught his eye in the first place.

He shaved the last patch of stubble away, rinsed his face in the basin, grabbed the towel. She brought a platter of bacon and eggs to the table, as Sergeant Major Gillespie's mouth watered. He tucked in his blue shirt emblazoned with three gold chevrons and three rockers on each sleeve. Shameful for a soldier to live with lace curtains and doilies, but he couldn't help it.

Across the table sat his wife, plump but still pretty. They ate in silence, their only son away at school, preparing for West Point. He had a good chance, because General Custer wrote a personal letter of recommendation, and Sergeant Major Gillespie won the Congressional Medal of Honor at Antietam.

"Hope there's no trouble with Benteen today," Sergeant Major Gillespie muttered, biting into a gingerbread muffin. "Enough hate on this post, you can cut it with a bayonet."

"Stay out of it," she replied, stirring her cup of coffee. "If officers want to fight, and you stop them, they'll both turn on you. Maybe if we're lucky they'll kill each other, and we'll get a new commanding officer."

Sergeant Major Gillespie and his wife were Old Army, not overly impressed by General Custer. The Boy General came up too fast, broke too many conventions, to suit them.

"I never seen such a worthless and silly bunch of officers in me life," Sergeant Major Gillespie said. "Before the war, that's when we had a real Army. We fought for the flag and the nation, but nowadays they just fight to git their names in the papers."

General Custer stood before the full-length mirror in his bedroom, tying his red bandanna. His hair was long and curly to his shoulders, mustache drooped to his chin. He put on his buckskin jacket and studied the effect with a critical eye. The Wolverines adored him during the war, but now his men despised him, laughed behind his back, and he was a sensitive man.

"You'd better hurry," Libbie said. "The troops are forming up."

He buttoned his buckskin jacket, carefully adjusted his wide-brimmed hat over his eyes. Then he took a step backward and examined the total effect.

"Don't let Benteen do anything to provoke you," she counseled. "He'll go too far and hang himself someday, all you have to do is let him. Just be patient, Autie. I have complete faith in you. One day soon, your time will come."

Stone opened his eyes. He lay on the floor of the guardhouse, had a severe headache, and wondered if his skull was cracked. He arose, staggered to the water bucket, drank some down.

He heard commands on the parade ground, the drum-out was under way. His head spun, he lost his balance, dropped to one knee near the water pail. He dipped the cup in, poured water over his head.

It refreshed him, he rinsed his mouth and swallowed it down. His stomach was hollow. If he didn't get a square meal pretty soon, he wouldn't make it.

He sipped water, heard more commands from the parade ground, roll of drums. The Seventh Cavalry band played the infamous "Rogue's March." He arose, dragged his ball and chain to the window.

Every soldier on the post was gathered in formation on the parade ground. The American flag on top of the pole whipped in the wind. In the center of the formation, a sturdily built captain with fluffy white hair and sideburns stood at attention, while out of the ranks marched the unfortunate wretch being drummed out.

In the bright morning sun, Captain Benteen watched Lieutenant Classen approach with fine crisp movements. Resentment rose in Benteen's craw, he was from the Volunteer Army, and didn't like West Point officers. Lieutenant Classen came to a halt in front of Benteen, saluted smartly. A faint smile on his face, Captain Benteen reached forward and tore off Lieutenant Classen's left shoulder board, flung it to the ground, stomped on it. Then he ripped off the right shoulder board.

The drumroll sounded, every man in the ranks stood ramrod straight. Custer watched from a position twenty feet behind Benteen, who pulled away Lieutenant Classen's sharpshooter medal, flung it over his shoulder. "I was in charge around here," he mumbled threateningly, "we'd draw and quarter you, you goddamned coward!"

General Custer said, "Just get on with it, Captain. We don't need a commentary."

Captain Benteen shot an angry look to General Custer, then pulled a pocketknife from his pants, opened the blade, took a shiny brass jacket button in his left hand, cut it off Lieutenant Classen's tunic. "I had my way, I'd cut your no-good throat!"

Lieutenant Classen's face showed no emotion, and it annoyed Captain Benteen that he was so firmly under control. "I ever see you outside this post, I'll put a bullet in your head."

A crowd of civilians from Fort Hays gathered in front of the orderly room, and Slipchuck was among them, with Daugherty the gambler, watching the show. Both were bleary-eyed and hung over. "You see that tall lieutenant in front of Troop D?" asked Daugherty.

Slipchuck turned his eyes in that direction, spotted the jaunty young red-haired officer who'd saluted him when Slipchuck first came to Fort Hays.

"That's Forrest, the one what put it to Major Scanlon's wife."

On the other side of the post, in a darkened room, Major Scanlon sat with a glass of whiskey in hand, unshaven, shirt half unbuttoned, a stain on his pants. He heard the drumroll, couldn't bear to watch the young man's misery. He sipped his glass of whiskey. If it weren't for General Custer's intervention, he'd be drummed out too. Major Scanlon smiled grimly, as drums rolled in the distance. *You can't court-martial a dead man.*

Captain Benteen sliced off Lieutenant Classen's final button, then unfastened the young officer's belt buckle, pulled the sword out of its scabbard, an inscription on the blade caught his eye:

To Ronald with love always
from Mother and Dad

"Congratulations," muttered Benteen. "You've made your parents proud of you."

Benteen saw the flicker of a smile on Classen's face. He removed the hat from Classen's head and threw it to the prairie wind that wafted it toward the horizon.

The drums continued their steady roll, like the crashing of surf on a beach. Captain Benteen drew back his arm and slapped Lieutenant Classen across the cheek. At that moment, Lieutenant Classen was expelled from the Army.

Captain Benteen took a step backward. Lieutenant Classen performed a left-face. The gate of Fort Hays lay straight ahead. His face like a statue, not the faintest inkling of an emotion showing, the former Lieutenant Classen moved his left foot forward as drums pounded.

All eyes were on him. His collar flapped in the breeze, trailing threads that had held insignia. His jacket hung open, buttonless, patches of white lining showing through tears in the fabric. General Custer was surprised and even heartened by Lieutenant Classen's proud performance. There was no stoop of shame in his shoulders, no falter to his step. He was leaving proudly, firm in his convictions. *So he's got guts after all. Good for you, boy. Don't let it get you down.*

Classen marched onward, and General Custer wondered what would happen to him. Might get a little dangerous in Hays City before the train arrived. Soldiers don't like cowards, and Classen wouldn't have the protection of the Army. Might find himself wishing he'd fought those injuns.

Captain Benteen seethed with fury as he watched Classen get away without a scratch. If he were commanding officer of Fort Hays, Classen would be found dead behind the stable, and the morning report would say the injuns got him.

Big black shadow at the front gate, clatter of hoofbeats, everyone turned toward a stagecoach drawn by six horses, crimson tassels on their harnesses. Two men sat on the seat with the driver, a third on the baggage compartment, strumming a banjo. The stagecoach passed through the gate and entered the fort. A pink silk-clad arm with jeweled bracelets hung out a stagecoach window, champagne glass in hand. Women's laughter could be heard as the high-stepping horses turned the stagecoach broadside to the parade ground.

Everyone stared in astonishment. It was a party on wheels, ladies and gentlemen dressed in the latest eastern fashions. One sweet young thing poked her pretty head out a window, stared wide-eyed at the formation of Seventh Cavalry, and giggled uncontrollably. A hoot went up from the carriage as a man's hand pulled her back inside.

The door opened and a tall, slim woman stepped to the ground. Classen advanced into the outstretched arms reaching toward him from the dark interior of the stagecoach. The woman slapped his butt saucily as he passed her, then she followed him in and closed the door.

The driver flicked his whip, the horses strained against their harnesses. The stagecoach moved toward the front gate. Officers and men from the Seventh Cavalry ogled with jaws agape as Lieutenant Classen leaned out the window and made an obscene gesture with his fingers toward Captain Benteen.

General Custer nearly folded with laughter. Captain Benteen sputtered, as his right hand dropped toward his service revolver.

"As you were, Captain!" General Custer shouted.

Captain Benteen's hand froze in midair. Everyone watched the stagecoach rumble through the gate; shrieks of laughter from the women could be heard in every trooper's ears. They imagined Lieutenant Classen lying on the floor with naked women, while they were still in the Army, forty miles a day on beans and hay.

The drum-out ended in a completely unpredictable way. Everyone stood at attention wondering what to do, except Sergeant Major Gillespie. "Sir," he whispered out of the corner of his mouth to General Custer, "I think it's time to dismiss the formation."

In matters such as parade-ground etiquette, General Custer always deferred to his sergeant major. He opened his mouth to give the command when a deep booming voice bellowed: *"Fannie!"*

The command caught in General Custer's throat. Had it been his imagination? He filled his lungs once more, when the name struck his ears again. *"Fannie!"*

He spun around. "Who said that!"

"I believe," replied Sergeant Major Gillespie, "it's comin' from the guardhouse."

"Get me out of here!"

General Custer strode toward the guardhouse, wide brim of his hat hiding his face in shadow. Sergeant Major Gillespie became confused for a moment, then pulled himself together and shouted: "Atten-*hut*! Dis-*missed*!"

The formation broke apart, Sergeant Major Gillespie followed General Custer, whose brow was furrowed, his profile like a hawk. He threw open the guardhouse door. Private Klappenbach leapt to attention behind the desk.

"Open the cell block!" General Custer ordered.

Private Klappenbach threw the bolt. Custer entered a vestibule and looked through the bars. A tall, powerfully built prisoner in a too-small uniform, face covered with beard, filthy from head to foot, stood in front of him.

"Don't you recognize me, Fannie?" the prisoner asked. "It's John Stone."

General Custer flashed on a smooth-faced young cadet in West Point uniform, captain of the lacrosse team, champion of the fencing team, they'd been friends and tipped many a mug together at Benny Haven's. "What the hell're you doing here?"

"A deserter robbed me and took my clothes. I've been in your guardhouse two days, and I haven't done anything."

"Free him!" General Custer declared.

Sergeant Buford sputtered, "But he killed a man!"

"He came at me with a knife," Stone explained. "It was him or me."

"I thought I said *free him*!" Custer gazed angrily at Sergeant Buford.

"But, sir, he's a deserter!"

"From where?"

"I don't know, sir."

"Sergeant Buford, you don't unlock that cell, I'll throw *you* in the guardhouse."

General Custer's mustaches quivered with tension, his eyes shot painful rays into Sergeant Buford's brain. "Yes, sir." Sergeant Buford unlocked the door. Stone lifted his ball and chains, shuffled out of the jail.

"Tell the blacksmith to fire up the forge, Sergeant Buford. We've got to take off that ball and chain. Let's not tarry. He's an innocent man."

"But he's wearin' an Army uniform, sir!"

"Even an idiot can see it's not his. I thought I told you to rouse the blacksmith. All you other men, clear out of here!"

They fled toward the door, the guardhouse was emptied in seconds. General Custer led Stone to the chairs. "I was camped on the prairie," Stone began, and told the story from pneumonia to the drum-out. "When I called your name, I didn't know if you could hear me. Thank God you did, because this is some guardhouse. Sergeant Buford is awfully free with that riding crop of his."

"Just what I need to keep the men in line. What're you doing in Kansas?"

"Do you remember my girlfriend from South Carolina, I used to talk about her all the time?"

"You ever marry her?"

"I've been looking for her since the war ended, been just about everywhere, followed a million wrong leads, and finally tracked her here, but now she's gone. Her name was Marie Higgins, and evidently she became Marie Scanlon."

General Custer's foot fell from the desk. "Are you sure they're both the same woman?"

Stone took the picture out of his shirt pocket and handed it to General Custer. "You tell me whether or not this looks like Marie Scanlon."

General Custer looked at the picture. "I were you, I'd forget her. She's trouble, you can take it from me. How'd your face get cut up?"

The door opened, Sergeant Buford thrust his head inside. "The blacksmith is ready, sir."

"Help Mr. Stone with that iron ball, will you, Sergeant?"

Sergeant Buford's eyes hooded with barely suppressed rage as he approached Stone and lifted the heavy iron ball. Chains dragged over the floor of the orderly room as Stone stepped toward the door. The fresh air hit him, he took a deep draught, soldiers in the vicinity watched curiously. The word had spread like wildfire across the post. One of Custer's old friends had been thrown into the guardhouse by mistake.

"Did you know the man Marie Scanlon left with?" Stone asked Custer.

"Derek Canfield, the gambler. Sleeps all day, up all night, hard drinker, talks a good game. Wasn't here that long. They knew each other before the war."

Stone racked his brain, but couldn't remember a Derek Canfield. Maybe he'd changed his name. He couldn't imagine Marie being with such a person. "Anything else you can tell me about her?"

"They say she had a romance with Lieutenant Forrest, executive officer of Troop D."

Stone swallowed hard. Didn't sound like the Marie he knew, but many years had passed and he'd changed considerably too. The chain pulled his arm. He turned to Buford, carrying the iron ball. Their eyes met and silent messages of hate passed between them. Stone was tempted to punch him in the mouth, but remembered his West Point training. Always plan your battle in advance, fight when you're ready, on the ground of your choosing, and once you commit yourself, pull out the stops.

The blacksmith worked the huge bellows, the fire roared. "Have a seat," he said to Stone.

Stone placed his left ankle on the anvil. He grit his teeth against the hammer's shock. The blacksmith raised his hammer, took aim. It landed with a loud *clank*; Stone felt the shock in the marrow of his bones.

"I guess I should congratulate you on your stars," Stone said to Custer.

"Everybody used to say you'd be the first to make general. By the way, what do you do for a living?"

"My last job was trail boss for a herd of longhorns, brought 'em from Texas to the railhead at Sundust."

"Ever tangle with injuns?"

The hammer came down again, Stone's brain was jarred in his skull, he lost consciousness for a split second. "Now yer hands," the blacksmith said.

Stone placed his hands on the anvil. "Tangled with them a few times."

"If you need a job, I could use another scout."

"I'll take it."

"You haven't asked how much it pays. Same old Johnny. What were you in the war?"

"Company commander."

Clang! Stone's teeth rattled, the cuffs fell off his wrists. He was unencumbered, a free man once more. He felt light as straw without the ball and chain. He faced Sergeant Buford. "We haven't seen the last of each other."

"Ready when you are," Sergeant Buford replied.

General Custer took Stone's arm. "Let's get you a bath, Johnny. You'll need new clothes, and you'll have dinner with my wife and me?"

John Stone walked across the parade field with General Custer, reflecting on the value of old West Point friendships. Without a powerful friend, man could rot and die in a military prison, be buried as a deserter, and no one would ever know.

"There's something I've got to talk with you about, Fannie," Stone said. "There's a man in the guardhouse who helped me, and I want to do something for him. He's sickly and might die, just because he spit in Captain Benteen's face. I know a trooper isn't supposed to spit in his commanding officer's face, but it's not serious enough to die for. His name's Antonelli. Can't you help him?"

"He's the worst soldier on the post, but if he spit in Captain Benteen's face, he can't be all bad. I'll see what I can do. Why don't you stop first at the sutler's, while I have an orderly draw you a bath. When you're finished with everything, come to my office."

Tomahawk walked alongside the strawberry roan toward a herd of wild horses grazing in the middle of a vast basin. Visible two miles away was an immense herd of wild buffalo. No humans in sight.

Freedom felt weird. Tomahawk shied as he drew closer to the herd. The strawberry roan reassured him with a comforting sound in her throat. Tomahawk could feel a strange power coming from the horses, different from the submissiveness of ranch horses. These brothers and sisters lived off the land, ran untrammeled, adjusted their lives to the twin cycles of sun and moon. They weren't the property of cowboys. They belonged to themselves.

Tomahawk drew closer, they made a path for him. A lifetime of captivity had made him a cautious creature. *Come join us,* they said. *We're headed for the land of the sun.*

He moved toward them, and they crowded around, rubbing against him, brushing him with their lips.

Stone walked toward the combination bar and sales counter in the sutler's store. The sutler arose from his chair, putting his newspaper to the side. "What can I do fer you?"

"Need civilian clothes."

The sutler was a crafty-faced bald man with long black sideburns. He looked Stone up and down, and Stone was a mess in his ragged, overtight, too-short uniform, surrounded by the stink of the jail, but he was a personal friend of General Custer. "Anything the gentleman wants," the sutler said unctuously with a little bow.

Stone heard something rustle behind him. He spun around, saw Captain Benteen sitting at a table in the corner. His eyes were large and bulged oddly, with a mean glint. Neither said a word, but Stone felt intense hostility coming from the officer. The sutler returned with an armful of clothes.

Stone picked a red shirt, and dark blue pants. He put on a pearl cowboy hat and looked in the mirror, but somehow it wasn't right. He missed his old Confederate cavalry hat, but the new one would have to do.

He heard footsteps behind him, two more officers entered the sutler's store. They strolled toward the table with Benteen, spurs jangling. Stone selected a brown cowhide belt with a plain brass buckle.

"Need a knife," Stone said.

The sutler dropped one on the counter. The blade was ten inches long, handle made of bone, carved with the figures of a turtle, horse, eagle, and lobo.

"Know what the carvings mean?" Stone asked.

"Ask the injuns who made it," the sutler replied. "They were Sioux."

One of the officers at the table said, "Honest soldiers get no credit, while the deserter gets an invitation to Iron Butt's house. Somebody ought to shoot the son of a bitch."

Stone dropped the belt on the counter, and looked at the officers. They had smirky, insinuating expressions, and Stone felt his temperature rise. He'd been on the dirty end of the stick for the past several days, and enough was enough.

He walked toward the table. Sarcasm on the officers' faces turned to surprise. Benteen half rose, hand moving toward his holster, but he couldn't shoot an unarmed man on a military installation, with witnesses. He let his hand fall. Stone came to the edge of the table. The officers got to their feet.

The sutler was sure his establishment would be damaged within seconds. He came out from behind his counter. "Please, gentlemen."

Stone made eye contact with each officer, then said, "Anybody wants to take a shot at me, take it now."

"You're not armed," said Benteen. "Strap on a gun, somebody might take you up on it."

Stone returned to the counter. "Colt with a holster."

The sutler disappeared into his back room. Stone glanced at the officers. Soldiering had changed since he was in the Confederate Army. Officers were gentlemen then. These were bullies with officers' shoulder boards.

The sutler placed a holster and gunbelt on the countertop, plus two guns. "Here's a Colt, but I thought you might want to look at this Starr Double Action. Has the advantage—you don't have to cock it."

Stone ignored the Starr. He didn't think a double action was as accurate as a single action. The Colt had hard use, blueing rubbed off the metal parts, wood grips smooth and dark, three notches cut below the trigger guard.

"Who owned it?" Stone asked.

"Was in a consignment shipped from Abilene. Lots of riflin' still in the barrel. Good shootin' condition, as you can see. Charge it to the general?"

Stone was sure his friend would understand. He loaded the gun, left the sixth chamber empty for safety purposes. Then he dropped it into his holster, adjusted the belt so the holster was in the correct intermediate position, tied the bottom of the holster to his leg.

The officers watched his every move. They were seasoned fighters, violence was their lives, and the stranger appeared ready to take on all of them. They weren't quite sure of how to proceed, for they were Army officers, not gunfighters.

Stone was ready, and his military background taught him to strike before the enemy could get ready. He walked toward the table, and the officers rose, moving their hands toward their guns. The sutler opened the window behind the counter and hollered: "Help!"

Stone stopped in front of the table, took a solid grip on the floor. "I've got a gun now," he said. "Who wants to go first?"

The officers looked at each other. They understood forward march, charge in echelons, retreat in an orderly fashion, this was something new.

Stone faced Captain Benteen. "How about you?" he asked. "You had a big mouth a few minutes ago."

Captain Benteen saw diamond-hard determination. Something told him to back off.

"I'm waiting," Stone said, eyes glittering in the light of the candle.

The officers hesitated. The man might be a gunfighter, and they wouldn't have a chance. The longer they looked at Stone, the more he was a professional. He was too sure of himself.

In a sudden move, Stone stepped forward. He pushed one officer out of his way, grabbed Captain Benteen by the front of his shirt, put him up against the wall. "You talk a lot, but that's about all."

Benteen's face turned red, eyes popped out. "You have me at a disadvantage. If I fight you on this post, your friend General Custer will court-martial me."

"Pick your spot."

"Behind the stable, after taps. Bare knuckle, just you and me, no weapons."

"Look forward to it," Stone replied. He walked to the counter, picked up his clothes, and headed toward the bachelor officers' quarters.

Slipchuck sipped a glass of whiskey at the bar of the Tumbleweed Saloon. He'd stayed at Fort Hays long enough to see Lieutenant Classen ride away, and been sick at heart ever since.

Always the other fellow who got fancy suits, pretty women, pink champagne, the easy life. You need money if you want to enjoy life. A poor man lives like a cockroach.

"You look like somebody just shot your horse," said a voice beside him.

Slipchuck turned to Daugherty, the gambler, sunlight glinting on the gold watch chain that covered his belly. "Sometimes life don't seem worth livin'," Slipchuck said. "A man works hard, what does he get? One day I'll keel over, that'll be the end of me, and I won't never have the things I always dreamed of."

"What is it you dreamed of?"

Slipchuck waved his arm wearily. "Oh, just the silly stuff goes on inside my poor ole head."

"The world is full of possibilities," Daugherty replied. "Tell me what you want, and who knows, maybe I can get it for you."

"How can you git it fer me, if'n you cain't git it fer yoreself?"

"If it's money you're talking about, I *can* and *do* get it for myself. Take a look at me. Do you think I'm poor?"

Slipchuck focused his old rheumy eyes on Daugherty, who wore a frock-coated suit, gold ring with big diamond, *mucho dinero.* "Are you really rich?" Slipchuck asked.

"I live in the best suite in the hotel. I eat the best food. And at night, I play cards. In case you haven't noticed, I don't lose often. Let's have a seat and talk business. Maybe you and me can do something for each other. Bartender, a bottle of your best, please, and if there's any steaks around, send two platters to that table over there."

Slipchuck followed the gambler to the table, they sat opposite each other. The bartender placed the bottle between them; Daugherty pulled the cork and filled Slipchuck's glass. Then he handed Slipchuck a stogie.

"Folks get suspicious if I win too much, because they know I'm a gambler. They figure I'm cheating, and I am. Now let me make a proposition to you. You're a smart man—I can tell by talking to you. I don't want to insult you, but you look like an old cowpoke down on his luck, and nobody'd ever suspect *you* of cheating. This is the way I see it: we sit at the same games, I feed you the cards, and you bet 'em." Daugherty winked. "You look like you been around a few poker games. You know what to do with a good hand, am I right?"

"I get the right cards, I know how to play 'em. But it's the other feller what always gits the ace-high straights."

"That's about to change, Slipchuck my friend. You and me, we split everything fifty-fifty. Maybe we should try it here tonight on a small scale, find out how it works."

"People seen us talkin'."

"Since when can't a man play cards with a friend? You want to fart through silk, this is your big chance."

"What if we get caught?" Slipchuck asked.

"Only fools get caught, and we're not fools."

Stone soaked in the hot bathtub, bits of dirt and dried blood loosening from his body, while his lice drowned en masse. Stone's eyes were closed and he felt almost normal again. An orderly brought a steak sandwich and a glass of milk. Stone wanted to lie in the tub for the rest of his life.

Marie had come and gone, he'd missed her by days, a rotten stroke of luck in a long line of catastrophies. According to everybody, she'd been screwing the troops. Well, not all of them. But enough to break his heart.

It wasn't the Marie he knew, the sweet, innocent girl who'd loved him so much. Well, maybe not that innocent. Marie had been nobody's fool. Ran off with a tinhorn gambler. Stone was anxious to get the full story from Major Scanlon.

He arose, lathered his face in the mirror, and shaved with the straight razor General Custer lent him. It was a painful job performed gingerly, due to the many bruises and contusions on his once-proud visage.

He rinsed his face, and dried it with a fluffy white towel. There was a knock on the door, and General Custer entered. The hero of Gettysburg looked at a tall, bruised cowboy, strapping on a gunbelt.

"Charged some weaponry to your account," Stone said. "Hope you don't mind."

"A man needs to be armed," General Custer replied. "Did you get a rifle? You'll need one. Pay me back when you get the money."

"Might not be for a long time."

"Go to the orderly room and tell Sergeant Major Gillespie to put you on the payroll."

"First I want to speak with Major Scanlon, if you don't mind. It's kind of important."

"Libbie's expecting you for dinner. Don't keep her waiting."

They left the cabin. Stone made for officers' row. Now at last he'd find out what happened to Marie. Stone hoped Major Scanlon was sober, but if not, Stone would sober him up. Stone had traveled too far, suffered too much, to be put off now.

Tomahawk walked at the rear of the herd, heading south toward the land of the sun. It was a bright cloudless day, with plenty of green grass and water every few miles, but soon demon winter would be there. A horse could starve or freeze to death.

The strawberry roan jacked her head up and down, always in his line of vision. No longer would Tomahawk spend nights tied to the hitching posts of noisy saloons, while John Stone drank himself into a stupor. Never again would he be awakened in the middle of the night, and expected to run at full gallop while other two-leggeds shot at him.

Movement caught Tomahawk's eyes. At the head of the herd, the leaders broke into a trot. No danger, doing it for fun, the rest of the herd surged forward, straining against the wind, gathering speed over the open range.

Tomahawk loved to run unrestrained by a saddle and heavy John Stone. He loosened his muscles and shook his head, his long black mane trailing behind him. The churning breeze whistled past his ears, a stream of saliva flew from his mouth into the air. He examined the ground carefully in front of him, wary of holes that could break a horse's leg at the knee. The herd spread out, so fewer horses would eat dust. It became a race among the males, showing off for the females.

Tomahawk hadn't been ridden hard for several days. He turned to see the strawberry roan behind him, observing his form. The only thing to do was turn it on.

Tomahawk filled his lungs with air, reached for more prairie. Horses in front veered to the side as he passed among them, his mouth unfettered by a painful bit. He was free, it felt better with every passing moment.

He thundered toward the front rank of horses, where the herd's leaders held their positions. They heard him coming, glanced nervously behind them. Tomahawk neighed as he came abreast, gobbling up sod with long strides. Inch by inch he pulled ahead, his heart pounding like a drum as he led the wild ones to Mexico.

Stone approached a two-story cottage on officers' row. The sign on the door said MAJOR ROBERT SCANLON. Windows were shuttered though it was only midafternoon. This was where Marie lived until a week ago. Stone stepped forward and knocked.

There was no answer. He hitched up his gunbelt, took out his bag of tobacco, rolled a cigarette. Then he knocked again. Silence came from within the house. Had Scanlon gone out, or was he passed-out drunk inside? Stone puffed the cigarette, looked toward the parade ground, where men snipped the grass. At the other end, a squad practiced close-order drill. A luckless private ran around the parade ground, carrying a full pack on his back and his rifle in his hands high over his head, shouting something Stone couldn't hear precisely.

Stone turned the doorknob; it was locked. He hoped Scanlon hadn't gone over the hill, with his valuable information about Marie. Stone walked toward the rear door of the house, feeling out of balance. He was accustomed to two guns, which provided a six-bullet added margin of safety. He'd buy another Colt soon as he received his first pay.

He came to the back door, knocked, again no answer. Glancing about, he saw children playing in a yard nearby. He reached down and turned the doorknob. It opened. Stone slipped silently into a small kitchen.

He felt Marie's emanations immediately. This had been her kitchen, no mistake about it. A chill crept up Stone's back. The tub in the sink was filled with dirty dishes and glasses. The reek of stale whiskey was in the air, empty bottles everywhere. Stone entered a passageway, came to the living room. A man with graying hair and a mustache sprawled on the sofa, clothes rumpled and stained.

Stone bent over him, shook his shoulder. "Major Scanlon?"

A sigh escaped the major's lips, his eyelashes fluttered. Stone shook him harder. The major grumbled in his sleep, rolled over, faced the back of the sofa. Stone looked at the crisscrossed suspenders on the major's back. He didn't come through five years of hell to be put off by a drunkard.

He returned to the kitchen, worked the pump, filled a bucket with cold water. Then he carried the bucket to the living room and dumped it over the head of Major Scanlon.

The provost marshal of Fort Hays felt as though he'd been plunged headfirst into a river. He sputtered, coughed, rolled over, saw a tall, brawny cowboy standing in the middle of the living room, wide-brimmed hat on his head, cigarette dangling out the corner of his mouth.

Major Scanlon raised himself to a sitting position on the sofa, wondered if he was hallucinating. "Who the hell're you?" he asked.

"John Stone."

There was silence for a few moments as both men examined each other. "You're not dead?" Major Scanlon uttered.

"Not yet. Mind if I sit down?"

"Can I get you something (burp) to drink?"

"I've come a long way, and I wonder if you'd be kind enough to answer a few questions about Marie."

Major Scanlon's gaze faltered. The muscles of his face sagged in misery. "Are you the John Stone that she . . . ?"

"I was supposed to marry her, but she was gone when I returned home after Appomattox. She left with you?"

"You weren't killed at Sayler's Creek?"

"Not as far as I know."

"That's what she heard. It wasn't much fun playin' . . . second fiddle to a ghost, only . . . are you sure you're John Stone?" Major Scanlon blinked his eyes in befuddlement.

"What made her think I was dead?"

"It's what somebody told her, right after her mother died in the Siege of Columbia. I found her living in the open with some other people. She was half-crazy with grief over the both of you, and scared to death. I thought she was a beautiful lady in distress, I'd read my Sir Walter Scott, you see. So I helped her, ended up marrying her, brought her west with me." Major Scanlon closed his eyes, and tears ran down his cheeks. "But she never loved me."

"She must've felt something, if she came with you."

"She needed a man to lean on, and I happened along at the right time." With a rough gesture, Major Scanlon reached for the jug of whiskey sitting on the floor in front of the sofa. "So you're alive. Isn't that a kick in the ass?" He pulled the cork out, leaned back his head, drank some down. Then he held out the jug to Stone and shook it. "Sure you don't want a swallow? You might need one, after I finish with you."

"I don't drink," Stone said, tempted by the slosh in the whiskey jug. "Do you know where Marie went?"

"Never told me, never even said good-bye. You might want to ask Lieutenant Forrest. They were quite . . . friendly."

Stone looked at the room where she'd lived. Now he knew why she'd left no message for him in South Carolina. Corpses can't read, and that's what she thought he was. Now the pieces fell into place. "Did she speak of me often?"

"Too damn often. She told me one night you were . . . the only man she ever loved."

He'd believed it five years. It led him across the length and breadth of the frontier. Now at last he knew it was true, but couldn't imagine whether to laugh or cry. Major Scanlon raised the jug to his lips, his Adam's apple bobbled, whiskey spilled down his chin. His eyes were red and baggy, his complexion sallow, ready to give up the ghost.

"You poor son of a bitch," Stone said.

"I don't want your pity," Major Scanlon replied, turning down the corners of his mouth. "She was mine, or almost mine, for a little while. My troubles be over soon, but what're *you* going to do?"

Stone walked toward the orderly room, overjoyed to know that Marie still loved him. Now all he had to do was track her down, but where the hell was she? The more he thought about it, the more he was sure he didn't know Derek Canfield. Maybe she'd met him while Stone was away in the war.

He came to the sutler's store, licked his lips. A glass of whiskey to steady him, but it was never just one. In the last town, a friend had been shot due to Stone's drunkenness, and Stone swore never to touch another drop. He looked at the flags in front of the orderly room. Work a few months, save his money, resume his search for Marie. He squared his shoulders and walked past the sutler's store. A man's sardonic laughter came to him from one of the windows, but Stone didn't turn around. How strange that Marie lived on this very post and transversed these same paths.

He entered the orderly room, Sergeant Major Gillespie looked up from his desk.

"I'm the new scout," Stone said.

"Yer name?"

"John Stone."

Once again the name rang in Sergeant Major Gillespie's brain, and repetition paid off. "Somebody's been in here lookin' fer you."

"Old feller?" Stone placed his hand at chest level. "About this tall?"

" 'At's him," said Sergeant Major Gillespie.

"Where'd he go?"

"Didn't say, but if I had to guess, try the hog pens."

"Where's Lieutenant Forrest?"

"Company D."

Stone left the orderly room. A big black stallion hitched to the rail reminded him of Tomahawk. It was the first time Stone thought of his trusty mount since he got out of jail. What happened to poor Tomahawk?

The animal did anything asked of him, always gave one hundred percent. A shame if injuns got him, but they wouldn't eat him. He was too fine an animal. Stone wondered how Tomahawk would handle a warrior on his back.

Stone never treated Tomahawk well, but hadn't been much better to himself. Should've bought apples and cubes of sugar for Tomahawk once in a while, instead of drinking all that whiskey like a fool.

He came to the Company D orderly room. The first sergeant, a white-haired old trooper who looked like he should've retired

years ago, looked up from a list of requisitions.
"I'd like to find Lieutenant Forrest," Stone said.
"Supply room," the first sergeant replied.
Stone strolled outside into the late-afternoon sun. A squad of troopers on horseback rode by, jangling equipment and the creak of leather reminded Stone of the war. He walked through an alley to a crudely planked building behind Company D headquarters. The supply sergeant read an old newspaper at his desk.
"I'm looking for Lieutenant Forrest," Stone said.
"Who the hell're you?"
The two men stared at each other, then the supply sergeant arose behind his desk. He was the same height as Stone, but fifty pounds heavier, big beer belly.
"Out of my supply room," the sergeant said, "or I'll throw you out."
"Try it."
The supply sergeant advanced. Stone raised his fists. A voice said, "At ease." The tall, young, red-haired officer at the rear of the supply room said, "I'm Lieutenant Forrest. Who might you be?"
"John Stone."
Forrest hesitated. "Fight or talk?"
"Talk."
The supply sergeant stared at Stone with an expression that said: *I'm going to kick your ass someday.*
"Anytime," Stone replied.
Lieutenant Forrest sauntered toward the door. "Come to my cottage. We'll be alone there."
Stone followed him out of the supply room. Lieutenant Forrest had an aquiline nose and the full petulant lips of a child, plus a lanky ambling gait. "Heard you were on the post," he said. "Figured you'd stop by before long. Thought you might want to shoot me."
"I want information about Marie. Where the hell'd she go?"
"If I tell you, don't let Scanlon know. She doesn't want him following her."
"You have my word."
"San Francisco, but maybe they changed their minds since I talked with her last. If you ever find her, come up on her real easy. She thinks you're beneath six feet of Virginia."

"You ever meet Canfield?"

Lieutenant Forrest nodded.

"What's he look like?"

"Six feet, sickly looking, coughed a lot. Black mustache startin' to go gray."

Stone couldn't place him. Lieutenant Forrest opened the door to his cottage, took out a bottle and two glasses.

"Don't drink," Stone said, gazing with desire at the bottle.

Lieutenant Forrest poured himself two fingers, threw his campaign hat onto a peg, and his thick burnished hair caught the last rays of sunlight streaming through the windows.

Stone sat on the sofa, Lieutenant Forrest dropped onto a chair. Outside, the bugler blew retreat. The staccato music reminded Stone of West Point. Live by the bugle, die by the bugle.

Lieutenant Forrest sipped whiskey. "She talked about you a lot. I'd say she was obsessed with your memory. She never loved me, and we both knew it. We were just . . ."

"If only she stayed one more week."

"Couldn't take it anymore. Was at the breaking point."

"Sounds like she confided in you quite a lot."

"She needed somebody to talk with. Wasn't the most popular person on the post."

A powerful thirst for whiskey forced Stone to gaze at the bottle on the coffee table. All he had to do was reach over and take a drink.

"Did Marie have any other men on this post?"

Lieutenant Forrest laughed sardonically. "I'm sure a lot of them wished it, but I don't think so. Marie was rather straightlaced underneath her bluff exterior."

Stone took out her picture. "This is what she looked like when I knew her."

Lieutenant Forrest smiled faintly. The setting sun rimmed his profile in gold; he resembled a cherub in an Italian Renaissance painting. "Hasn't changed much. Maybe a few more pounds. A beautiful woman, no question about it."

It was dark when Stone knocked on General Custer's door. Eliza, the maid, opened it and looked him up and down. "You must be John Stone. The general's been talkin' 'bout you all night. Was he ornery when he was young?"

"Worse than now," Stone said, handing her his new cowboy hat.

She led him into the living room. General Custer rose to his feet, wearing fringed buckskin pants and a blue Army shirt without insignia. On the other side of the room, an exquisite woman sat near the fireplace, attired in a high-necked green velvet dress and black boots. Her hair was lustrous dark brown, a book in her hands.

General Custer bowed slightly. "My wife, Elizabeth Bacon Custer. I'd be in a gutter someplace, if it weren't for her."

She curtsied, held out her hand. Stone took it and bowed as though in the drawing room of his family's home before the war.

"Most people call me Libbie," she said. "Have a seat—may I call you Johnny? So you went to West Point with Autie? I'll bet you could tell me interesting stories about his time there."

"He won't," General Custer said, "on penalty of the firing squad."

"Autie said you were engaged to marry Marie Scanlon? How odd."

"Did you know Marie well?"

"I knew her, but couldn't say how well. I had no idea she'd run off with Derek Canfield. He's about as far from Lieutenant Forrest as you could get. Derek Canfield is a sick man. Isn't that so, Autie?"

"You smoked and drank as much as Canfield, you'd cough too."

Stone asked, "What was he doing at Fort Hays?"

"Came to see Marie Scanlon, what else?" Libbie replied.

The black maid entered the room. "Supper's ready."

Libbie took Stone's hand, led him to the dining room. A brace of plovers and haunch of antelope sat on the table, filling the air with mouth watering fragrance. Pots of sweet potatoes and regular potatoes were nearby. They sat, Libbie said a brief prayer, General Custer carved the antelope, Stone looked at Custer's knobby red hands. He'd always been an awkward soldier, earned more demerits than anyone in the class, graduated last, restless energy. Now he was the same rambunctious boy bent under the weight of command, and Libbie had him wrapped around her little finger.

She was a great beauty, with magnificent hair, dressed at the height of fashion, immaculately groomed, the kind of woman a man would want to keep him interested in life.

"What was your unit during the war?" General Custer asked, holding up the platter of meat.

Stone selected a thick savory slice and lay it on his plate. "The Hampton Legion."

"What rank did you attain?"

"Captain."

There was silence for a few moments. Libbie passed him the potatoes. "We don't get a variety of vegetables here," she explained apologetically. "We're at the end of nowhere. Prices are sky-high."

"I thought the Army could get anything it wants."

General Custer shook his head sadly. "Congress and the President keep military appropriations down, because nobody wants to pay taxes. Quite frankly, the men's food is terrible. If I were an enlisted man, I'd desert too. They're paid practically nothing, compared to what civilians earn in this area."

"They work so hard, and suffer so much," Libbie said. "They're the best men in America."

Stone gazed into her almond eyes. Fannie Custer had found himself one hell of a woman, but her view of the troopers was at variance with his. The Boy General didn't challenge her. He'd attack the Sioux nation with a handful of potential deserters, but avoid confrontations with his little wife at all costs.

General Custer turned to his former classmate from the old days. "I must confess my surprise you only became a captain, Johnny. Most of the men in our class did far better than that, and you were a friend of Wade Hampton's, weren't you? What happened?"

Stone sliced into his antelope steak. He normally didn't like to speak of these things, but the man was his host and a dear old friend. "It was all I could do to handle my company."

"You doubted yourself. So did I, sometimes. But I never let it stop me. I was a damn sight better'n the other hacks and charlatans with stars on their shoulders. But maybe you were the smart one. You did your duty and got out when it was over. Sometimes I wish I got out too. I've had opportunities, let me tell you. But I love the Army, and somebody's got to defend the people out here."

There was a knock at the front door, and a few moments later the black maid entered the dining room. "General," she said, "Sergeant Major Gillespie wants to speak with you."

General Custer wiped gravy from his mustache as he left the dining room. Stone welcomed the opportunity to be alone with Libbie. "Were you on friendly terms with Marie?" he asked, trying to draw her out.

"She made it difficult. I feel sorry for her, but I feel even sorrier for Major Scanlon. The poor man is finished."

"What did you think of Canfield."

"Not much to look at, but quite a charmer. Some officers spread the rumor that Autie was one of Marie's lovers. They'll say anything to discredit him. Petty men, they'll come to a petty end."

"Not all are that way, fortunately," General Custer said, returning to the dining room. "I have many good officers, and a few worthless backbiting sons of bitches. They resent me and do their best to subvert and undermine everything I do. I wouldn't put anything past them. They want to get ahead not by their merits but by dragging somebody down. They've met their match this time. I won't give in to them. They'll have to kill me, to get me out of the way."

Stone replied, "Ran into a few of them in the sutler's store, nearly came to lead."

"Did one of them have a round face, bug eyes, white hair?"

"That's him."

"Captain Benteen, worst of the lot. The man hates me with maniacal passion. If I could get rid of him, the morale of this post would increase one hundred percent. I don't know what I ever did to him, but it must've been pretty bad."

"You didn't do anything," Libbie said, placing her hand on his. "It's just the hatred an ordinary man feels in the presence of his betters. He's jealous, that's all."

"What's his background?" Stone asked.

"Citations for bravery, steadily promoted throughout the war. Recommended for the brevet rank of general, but didn't get it. I was recommended, and did get it. I think that's at the core of the problem. He's also five years older than I, and nobody likes to take orders from a younger man. A group of officers have gathered around him, and their main goal is harassing yours truly."

"I'm sure you can take care of yourself," Stone said. "You've General Sheridan on your side, if a man can believe what he reads in the papers."

"Depends on the papers, but General Sheridan and I are friends, thank goodness. One of these days I hope to convince him to send Benteen to China. If I win a significant victory against the injuns, he'll do anything I ask. But the politicians can't figure out what to do about the injuns. Some think we should conquer them and get it over with, others say we should send them to college and turn them into scholars. Liars and four-flushers've been debating it in Congress for nearly two years. If they ever turn the Seventh Cavalry loose, I'll wipe the injuns off the face of the earth."

"I know they've committed atrocities," Stone said, "and they've even killed friends of mine—hell—they've just about killed *me* a few times, but all they've got to look forward to is a reservation where they'll live on the starvation level for the rest of their lives, guarded by soldiers who despise them, and traders'll kill them with whiskey, for the almighty dollar. I was on the losing side of a war. I know how the injuns feel."

"You ever see a massacre?" Custer asked.

"Quite a few."

"I know the injuns been mistreated, but that doesn't give them the right to kill women and children, torture people, and mutilate them. They've got to learn to live at peace with the rest of us, or else."

Stone didn't like to argue about injuns. Everybody had his position, and nobody changed his mind. "If you had your choice, where'd you like to be posted?"

"New York City. Ever been there? Marvelously stimulating. A man can make a lot of money in New York."

"Why don't you resign your commission and go there?" Stone asked. "Fort Hays isn't exactly the garden spot of America."

"Don't want to spend the rest of my life in an office. I need the open land, fresh air, the feeling you get when you're riding where no white man has ever been."

"Speaking of garden spots," Stone added, "that guardhouse of yours should win a special prize. Did you take care of Antonelli?"

"He'll be sent to the hospital in the morning. I've already issued the order."

"He might make a good soldier. The loyal type. During the war, some of the most unlikely men became first-class soldiers. I was in awe of their day-to-day courage."

"They were good because of your leadership, Johnny. You knew how to get the best out of them."

"They didn't do it for me. They did it to save their families and their way of life, and they did it for Bobby Lee. If men believe what they're fighting for, all you have to do is explain what they have to do. They'll go out and wage war with everything they have."

"I don't believe in telling them anything," Custer said. "I don't want to confuse them. Not good for a soldier to think too much. I want them to obey commands the moment they're given. That's what I'm working for here. The men don't care about injuns the way the Wolverines cared about the Union. Quite a different situation. The primary ambitions of men on this post are whiskey and the hog pens. They expend more energy avoiding work than actually doing it. They have no sense of pride in anything, least of all themselves or their unit. And then there's Major Reno. About the only thing Captain Benteen and I agree on is Major Reno. The man's an idiot through and through. You remember Reno, don't you? Jimmy Whistler's friend?"

"Good God, is Reno here too?"

"In the flesh. The most indecisive and confused man in the world. Wherever he goes, the cloud of gloom follows. Yet here he is, on this very post, my second in command. I tell you—the dregs of the world are congregated here at Fort Hays, and I must be the dregs myself, because I'm their commanding officer."

Libbie turned to her dinner guest. "Don't let him continue like this, Johnny. I feel as if I'm sinking in a sea of black ink."

General Custer threw his hand in the air. "What's the use of trying, when nobody gives a damn? Maybe I should've accepted one of those offers in New York when I was there, but it's not too late, maybe I will yet. An office in a nice building on Wall Street, my club around the corner, the opera, the theater, why do I stay here?"

"I have no idea," Stone said. "I'm leaving for San Francisco soon as I can."

Libbie gazed at Stone's fine profile. His nose looked slightly bent out of shape. She noted strong cheekbones, firm jaw, dreamy eyes, beneath numerous scars and bruises. Not a bad-looking man, in a rough sort of way. "What'll you do if you find Marie in San Francisco, Johnny? Will you try to take her away from Derek Canfield?"

"She'll join me of her own free will."

"What if she tells you to go away?"

"She won't."

"You're awfully sure of yourself."

"Till she tells me otherwise, I'm a-gonna keep on coming."

5

SLIPCHUCK STOOD AT the bar of the Tumbleweed saloon, sipping whiskey. It was night, the saloon jam-packed, card games going full blast at several tables. Nobody paid any special attention to Slipchuck, another face in the crowd.

He looked at the big round table where Daugherty played poker. Daugherty had been at it an hour, winning some, losing others, breaking even overall. As soon as an empty seat opened at the table, Slipchuck would take it.

Cheating didn't come easy to him, but at least he wouldn't handle the deck. That was Daugherty's job. Slipchuck wanted to win a big stake, live like a king for once in his life, dress like a dandy, screw until he dropped in his tracks, but he couldn't think of a better way to go.

A short man in a stovepipe hat arose from the table. Slipchuck moved through the crowd. "Mind if'n I sit down?"

"Come on," said a man in a black vest. "You got money to lose, make yerself comfortable."

Slipchuck glanced at Daugherty a few chairs away. The slick gambler wore his derby tilted forward, puffed a stogie. The air was a fragrant blue cloud that scratched the back of Slipchuck's throat. A farmer dealt the cards.

Slipchuck played conservatively, waiting patiently for the deck to circle the table and come to Daugherty. He studied the other gamblers: businessmen, cowboys, farmers, one professional gambler complete with diamond stickpin on his shirt, and the old stagecoach driver of the plains.

Slipchuck felt a moral qualm. Cheating wasn't fair, like shooting a man in the back. Slipchuck tried to swallow it down, justify, forget. Everybody was cheating, from the Indian agent who stole food from women and children, to the businessman who shipped rotten beef to the Army, to the cowboy who burned a new brand over an old one. Slipchuck decided it was time to get his share. He'd been a straight shooter too long. The deck came to rest in Daugherty's hands. "Draw poker, and the joker is wild."

He shuffled the deck with fast hands, stacked it the way he wanted, palmed a card, dealt. Some cards came off the top, some off the bottom, but nobody detected anything in the smooth practiced movements of his manicured hands. The diamond ring on the third finger of his right hand sprayed a rainbow of light at the ceiling.

Slipchuck picked up his cards. Two aces and two trays, with the five of hearts. The farmer to the left of Daugherty opened, Slipchuck threw his coins into the pot. He tossed down the five, took one card, turned it up.

Another ace, producing a full house. In an ordinary game, Slipchuck would consider it an extraordinary stroke of luck, but instead he felt like a sinister demon. There was no joy when he placed his bets. Coins dropped into the pot, which grew to ten dollars, one third of a cowboy's pay for a month. Then the air became too rarified for some. One by one they dropped out. Even Daugherty folded his hand. Finally it was Slipchuck and a corporal with the top three buttons of his blue tunic unbuttoned. The corporal called Slipchuck but didn't buck him. Slipchuck concluded the corporal was reaching the limits of his resources. Slipchuck matched his bet and raised him again.

"Must be a helluva hand you got there," the corporal said suspiciously. "Wonder if you're bluffin'."

"One way to find out," Slipchuck replied.

The corporal put a five-dollar coin on the table. Slipchuck knew he had him hooked. If he increased the bet, the corporal would keep going until he had no money left. A corporal wasn't rich, Slipchuck didn't want to clean him out. He tossed five dollars onto the pile, turned over his cards.

The corporal stared at them, his features sagging like melted butter. Then he showed his own cards, three queens and two tens. A strong hand, but not strong enough. Robbery with a deck of cards.

Slipchuck pulled the mountain of coins toward him. The corporal grumbled as he left the table.

"A man shouldn't play cards," somebody said, "he can't afford to lose."

Slipchuck wanted to walk away from the game, but you can't if you just won big. The deck passed to the next man. Slipchuck tossed his ante into the pot. He sipped whiskey, tried to think about the fun he'd have with the money. A man could live high on the hog. Buy a carriage and a fancy horse. Check into the best hotel in town. He glanced toward the bar, where the corporal stared sullenly into his glass of whiskey. Slipchuck lost many big pots in his day. *About time I won a few.*

Stone arrived behind the stable, no one else there. He wondered if Captain Benteen had changed his mind about the fight. He decided to wait. Plenty to think about. He sat on a wagon and looked at Orion the warrior in the starry heavens. Had Marie gone to San Francisco, or was it a ruse? Who was Derek Canfield? What about Fannie Custer?

It was discomforting to see his old friend again. They'd been in the same class at West Point, suffered the same humiliations from upperclassmen and professors. Now Custer was a famous war hero and Indian fighter, while Stone had plenty of nothing at all.

What happened to me? He'd shown promise when he was young, everyone said. Even Custer thought Stone would be first to make general, but a weakness in Stone appeared during the early battles of the war. The slaughter bothered him. He couldn't order thousands of men to charge the mouths of Yankee cannon from a safe position behind the lines. The carnage was too great, but real fighting generals like Custer never hesitated. So Stone remained an ordinary company commander, despite entreaties from Jeb Stuart and Wade Hampton to move up the chain of command. He never wanted to see men as pawns on a chessboard, and that's what high command made you do.

He heard voices. Men approached through the alley, Benteen came into view. "I'll be damned. Son of a bitch showed up."

Three officers were with him. Benteen took off his hat, stripped off his shirt, gave the impression of raw power. Stone dropped his hat and shirt into the wagon. Then he faced Benteen. The three officers stood to the side, campaign hats cocked at odd angles on their heads. They'd been drinking and were in a fine mood.

"Kick his ass," one of them said to Benteen. Another laughed, and the third hitched his thumbs in his gunbelt. "I bet he's a runner," he said. "Any friend of General Custer's would have to be."

Stone pointed his finger at the officer. "You're next."

The officer replied, "You're headed for the doctor's office."

"Ready?" Benteen asked, hammering his right fist into his left palm. He bent his knees, raised his dukes, advanced cautiously. Stone watched for telltale signs that telegraphed punches and revealed style. *Figure him out, you've got him beat.*

Benteen continued to move forward, and Stone slipped to the side, showed him angles, looked for clear paths. He threw a tentative jab to Benteen's chin, and Benteen picked it off in midair. Stone jabbed Benteen's stomach, and Benteen swept the punch to the side with his forearm. Horses whinnied and neighed inside the stable, disturbed by sounds of conflict outside.

Stone threw another jab at Benteen's nose, and Benteen leaned back, then counterpunched suddenly. Stone's forehead was in the way, and Benteen's fist crashed into it. Stone saw stars for a moment, Benteen followed with a right cross that landed squarely on Stone's left cheekbone.

Stone took two steps backward, but appeared no worse for wear. Benteen was dismayed. The three officers looked at each other in surprise. The full weight of Benteen's body went into the punch, but hadn't affected Stone at all. *He must be faking,* thought Benteen, veteran of many wars. *Maybe if I go after him . . .*

Benteen hurled a left jab to Stone's chin, but Stone hooked Benteen on the nose. Benteen saw the white light for a split second. A trickle of blood appeared at the end of his nostril, and made him mad.

He waded into Stone, throwing punches from all angles, trying to take him out quickly. Stone caught most of the punches on his arms and wrists, twisting and turning, giving plenty of head movement, waiting for Benteen to open himself up.

Benteen feinted, and Stone fell for it. A fist came flying over the top, smacked Stone on the left eye. It was a jarring blow, and when he raised his arms to protect his upper body,

Benteen hooked his left kidney, right kidney, slam-bang pinwheels of light.

Stone looked up, and Benteen stood over him, fists balled. Stone shook his head, tried to clear it, and Benteen kicked him in the face. The force of the blow sent Stone tumbling over. He struggled to regain his balance, and Benteen kicked him in the chest, knocking him onto his back. Benteen jumped with both feet onto Stone's head, but Stone rolled out at the last moment and scrambled to his feet. Benteen turned around and saw a fist directly in front of his eyes.

It connected with Benteen's forehead, and Benteen felt as if the stable had fallen on him. He staggered, his knees buckled, and the only thing for Stone to do was hit him again.

Stone planted his feet firmly and took him apart with a ceaseless flow of carefully aimed punches. Benteen backpedaled, tried to protect himself, dodged and ducked, but his timing was off, most of Stone's blows got through. Cartilage crackled in Benteen's nose, his teeth rattled loose in his throat, his left eye puffed up like a balloon, but he wasn't ready to go down.

Through bleary, fuzzy eyes Benteen watched Stone advance. *Maybe I can make him reach.* Blows rained on Benteen as he took long, unsteady steps backward. Stone moved after him, and Benteen threw an uppercut as Stone came in, connecting with the bottom of Stone's chin. Stone's head snapped up, Benteen fired a powerful jab into Stone's belly. Stone expelled air, went into a crouch, Benteen slammed him on the side of his head, but Benteen's timing had never fully recovered. Stone threw a straight jab up the middle, and connected with Benteen's mouth. Benteen tasted blood on his tongue, saw a vague blur near his left eye, everything went black. Benteen dropped to one knee. He shook his head, blood dripped freely from his nose and mouth, and Stone stood over him.

Benteen couldn't let General Custer's schoolboy friend defeat him. He pushed his legs and rose to an upright position, raising his fists to protect himself.

Stone stepped forward, picking his shots. The accumulation of sharp accurate punches wore Benteen down, his efforts to defend himself became more clumsy, he could launch no offensive of his own, it was only a matter of time.

A right hook to the ear did it. Captain Benteen collapsed like a sack of flour at Stone's feet. Stone looked at him for a moment, stepped over his body, advanced toward the officer who'd insulted him.

The officer had a thin black mustache, and Stone had told him he was next. The officer didn't want to fight Stone with fists, after the exhibition he'd just witnessed. His hand lowered to his gun, but before he could open the flap of his regulation holster, Stone's Colt was aimed at his stomach.

The officer turned white with fear. He'd gone for his gun first, that made him fair game, he was going to die. He thought of his mother in Minneapolis, and the girl he left behind. Stone was in a rage. He wanted to put a hole through the arrogant bastard, but couldn't shoot a man in cold blood.

He walked away, leaving Benteen motionless on the ground, his three cohorts trying to slap and shake him awake. But their efforts were to no avail. Benteen would remain unconscious for the next half hour.

Sergeant Buford lay on top of the rise, rifle in his hands, looking at the Wakhatchie River crossing. It was a dark night, moon hidden by a patch of clouds blowing across the starry heavens.

Buford wore a blue service jacket with the collar buttoned, no chevrons or insignia to catch what little light was there. He looked for the shift of shadows that would indicate a rider's approach. Put a bullet between the damned drunkard's eyes, to hell with a duel. Scanlon wasn't worth the trouble. Buford had contempt for the provost marshal. No wonder his wife left him. The man was a disgrace to his uniform. A woman cheats on a man, shoot her. The only way to handle the bitches.

Buford heard hoofbeats, perked up his ears. From afar he heard the wail of a lobo. The moon rolled into an open region of the sky, illuminating a rider in the distance. Buford sighted down the barrel of his service carbine. He'd already adjusted sights for windage and distance. A man who couldn't control his wife deserved to die.

Sergeant Buford pasted his sights on Major Scanlon's chest, squeezed the trigger, the rifle fired. A bullet whacked into Major Scanlon, the shock jolting him loose from his roots. He slid out of the saddle and fell to the ground. Sergeant Buford ran down the hill, rifle in hand, to finish him off at close range. Sometimes men pretend to be dead, and Buford was ready for tricks. He slowed as he drew closer, aimed the rifle at Major Scanlon's head.

Major Scanlon lay on his back, his blue Army shirt covered with blood and rows of medals. The provost marshal wore a full dress uniform, and a faint smile.

"I knew I could . . . rely on you," Major Scanlon said through teeth rinsed with blood.

Sergeant Buford recoiled. Now he understood. Major Scanlon set Buford up to kill him, so he wouldn't have to do it himself. "You son of a bitch," Buford growled. "I hope you burn in hell."

Major Scanlon closed his eyes. Sergeant Buford aimed at his head, fired. Blood and brains flew in all directions. Sergeant Buford drew his knife and proceeded to mutilate Major Scanlon injun style.

Slipchuck sat behind a hundred dollars in coins, while Daugherty dealt another hand. It was after midnight, and Slipchuck wanted out of the game. He'd been playing for nearly three hours, the mental strain getting him down.

He could win this hand, but not by too much. You couldn't let them get suspicious. A man who dealt from the bottom of the deck, as Daugherty just did, could be shot on the spot, or lynched at dawn. The cheater's partner could expect no better.

Slipchuck sipped a glass of whiskey. Couldn't guzzle as he wanted. This wasn't a game of chance anymore. He tried to think of whores in silk underwear as he glanced at a poor farmer who'd been losing steadily all night, down to his last twenty dollars. *Drop out while you got a chance,* Slipchuck thought. *I'll take every penny you got.*

The poor farmer couldn't hear Slipchuck's thoughts. He studied the cards in his hand: six and seven, nine and ten, plus a tray. Could he fill the straight? He looked at the money in the pot. *Maybe I can bid it up, take it all home. The hand I've been waiting for all my life.*

Daugherty looked at him from beneath bushy eyebrows, puffing his stogie. He knew the farmer was a desperate man. You could see it in his eyes and every move he made.

A few chairs away, the man in the black leather vest watched Daugherty. Black Vest had smooth hands, and Daugherty pegged him for a professional too, but Daugherty was in the clear, since

Slipchuck was the winner, not he. He shuffled the cards, stacked them deftly, seven of clubs on the bottom.

"How many?" he asked the farmer.

The farmer pushed one card forward. Daugherty tossed him the seven of clubs, tried not to laugh when the farmer peeked at the corner. He'd done the impossible, filled an inside straight!

Slipchuck asked for two cards. Three soldiers at the table dropped out, three stayed in. Black Vest began the second round of betting. The farmer bucked him, another soldier folded, and Slipchuck stayed in, raising the farmer. Black Vest raised Slipchuck. The farmer bucked Black Vest. Slipchuck raised the bet once more. The last soldier dropped out. "Too rich for my blood," he said.

The betting continued, it was Black Vest's turn. He looked at his cards, glanced at Daugherty through thick blue smoke hovering over the table. "I'm out," Black Vest said, throwing his cards facedown on the table.

The farmer appeared on the verge of apoplexy. His clothes were ragged, he had the face of an abandoned dog, and he needed money, that was clear. Pay the bank or lose the farm, most likely.

"Five more dollars," the farmer said, twitching his nose, "and five to see you."

Slipchuck fingered coins. "Here's five, and I'll buck you ten more."

The coins jingled as they fell to the small mountain of wealth gleaming in the center of the table. The farmer looked at it, his eyes reflected the sparkle. All his worries would be over, if he could win that pot, and he held a straight with the nine high. "All I got left is ten dollars," he said. "I'll bet it all to see you."

He pushed his money forward, waited eagerly to see what Slipchuck had. Slipchuck fanned the cards in his hand and lay them down. The farmer stared at a flush of hearts. He pursed his lips and blew out a puff of air. "My God."

"You'll need more'n God," replied one of the soldiers. "A straight flush or better."

Slipchuck wrapped his arms around the pot, pulling it toward his end of the table. He had a grand total of nearly three hundred dollars, almost as much as he earned in the average year, but he'd never do it again. He wasn't cut out for cheating poor farmers. Slipchuck looked across the table, Daugherty winked. Slipchuck envied Daugherty for his fancy clothes and fast life, but not anymore. If there was hell, Daugherty surely would go there.

The farmer stared at his straight. He'd lost everything. Slipchuck scooped money into his pockets. "I been at this too long," Slipchuck said. "Time to take a break."

"But . . . but . . ." sputtered the farmer, "you got ter gimme a chance ter win me money back."

"You got nothin' to gamble with," Slipchuck replied, "and I had enough fer one night. Cain't hardly see the cards atall."

Slipchuck filled his shirt pockets. It was more than he'd ever had at one time in his life. The farmer stared at the diminishing pile, tears in his eyes. Slipchuck had a lump in his throat.

"Ain't it strange," said Black Vest. "The geezer wins whenever the dude was dealin'."

Deadly silence dropped over the table. Daugherty looked at him calmly. "You shouldn't make an accusation unless you've got proof."

"All I know is he won when you had the deck in yer hands."

"You shouldn't play, if you can't lose like a gentleman."

Black Vest drew himself to his feet. He wore faded tan britches, a green plaid shirt, his hatband made of silver disks with injun markings. His posture said he was a gunfighter. "Hard to lose like a gentleman when you're cheated."

It became quiet in the Tumbleweed Saloon. Gamblers, soldiers, drunkards, and idlers got out of the way. The man in the black vest looked ready to go the distance. Daugherty sat easily at the table, while Slipchuck stepped back and steeled himself for whatever might come.

"That there's Jess Pollard," said a voice at the bar.

Pollard stood taller at the mention of his name. Slipchuck had heard of him, hired gun from up Dakota way. *Lord,* Slipchuck prayed, *you get me through this, I'll never cheat at cards again.* Daugherty held the stogie at his mouth with one hand, moved his other hand into direct line with Pollard.

"I just called you a cheater," Pollard said. "Ain't you gonna do nothin' 'bout it?"

Daugherty replied, "You shoot me in front of these people, you'll hang."

The farmer looked at the pile of coins. It wasn't lost yet. "I seen 'em passin' signals to each other," he lied. "I want my money back."

"You think I cheated you," Slipchuck replied, "take it and git out'n my face." He turned to Pollard. "You too. I don't want yer money."

Pollard narrowed his eyes at Slipchuck. "Don't I know you from someplace?"

"I ain't seen you before, mister."

"You're the man what shot Frank Quarternight in the back."

"Never shot nobody in the back," Slipchuck said. "My name ain't Pollard."

Pollard stiffened, blood drained from his face, and Slipchuck knew it was the wrong thing to say. But Slipchuck had never walked away from a fight in his life. Pollard turned toward Slipchuck, and Daugherty made his move.

A derringer was up his sleeve, hooked to a spring. He scratched his shoulder, the tiny weapon popped into his right hand, carefully positioned for the shot. Pollard whipped out his Remington. Daugherty raised the derringer, a shot fired, he was struck on the throat by Pollard's bullet. Blood poured out Daugherty's mouth and nose, he leaned to the side. Pungent gunsmoke filled the air, Daugherty fell to the floor and didn't move. Pollard looked at Slipchuck. "Now it's you and me, old man. Do you want to go first, or should I?"

Slipchuck's reflexes had faded considerably since he was young. The old stagecoach driver had come to the end of his road.

"I just asked you a question, old man. Or has something happened to yer hearing? What you waitin' for?"

Slipchuck smiled grimly. At least he'd die like a young man, with a gun in his hand and his boots on, instead of in a hospital, with drool in his beard and cataracts on his eyes.

"I'm a-ready fer you," Slipchuck said, spreading his bony arthritic fingers, his body tensed for the final pull. "Make yer play."

They gazed at each other over the table piled high with coins. A gleam came to Pollard's eye when he thought of new glory accruing to his reputation. He tensed, licked his lips with the tip of his tongue, got ready.

"Hold on!" said a voice in the doorway.

Pollard and Slipchuck turned to the tall, husky figure silhouetted against the night sky.

"If you're going to shoot that old man," Stone said to Pollard, "you'll have to shoot me first."

Pollard guffawed out of the corner of his mouth. "Fine with me, cowboy. I'm takin' on all four-flushers and fools tonight."

Stone advanced toward the center of the saloon, and those on the floor took the opportunity to scramble out the front and back doors.

"I got no respect for a man who'd gun down an old fart," Stone said.

"Now hold on, Johnny," Slipchuck protested. "I ain't *that* old."

Stone took a position opposite Pollard. "You want gunplay, I'll give it to you."

Pollard didn't know the cowpoke, but people would laugh if he walked away now. "Give it to me," he said.

Stone's hand slapped the butt of his Colt, while Pollard's fingers darted toward his Remington. The saloon reverberated with the gunshot. The bartender cringed behind a keg of beer. Pollard's knees turned to jelly, he twisted to the side. His gun was halfway out of its holster, it weighed a ton. He tried to raise it higher, Stone fired again.

The bullet struck Pollard's heart, his lights went out, but his body didn't know it. He stood unsteadily for a few seconds, then crashed to the floor.

Stone stood still as a statue in the light of coal-oil lamps and candles, smoking gun in hand, the wide brim of his black cowboy hat casting a shadow over his face. Silence in the saloon, air bitter with gunsmoke. "Finished over there?" the bartender asked.

Stone holstered his gun. He looked at the nearest glass of whiskey, fought the evil impulse. Pollard lay on his back, blood poured out two holes, soaking his shirt and the surrounding floor. A few feet away, Daugherty lay in a crimson pool.

"Let's get out of here," Stone said.

Stone and Slipchuck walked out the back door. Sheds, privies, stacks of wood, could be seen in the moonlight. The prairie stretched spectrally to the horizon.

They strolled past outbuildings to the edge of town, sat cross-legged on the ground like a couple of injuns. Stone reached to his shirt pocket, took out his bag of tobacco. Slipchuck withdrew one of Daugherty's stogies.

"Got mixed up with a professional cardsharp," Slipchuck explained. "Tired of bein' a poor man."

"You want to go to San Francisco with me?"

"You ain't really a-thinkin' about it, are you?"

"I've been to the fort, found out Marie's gone to San Francisco. Custer gave me a job. I can leave in two months."

"You don't have to wait two months. I just won a big pot. We can go right now. Only thing is I cheated a poor farmer. I was a-thinkin' I should give it back."

"Then do it. I'll get you a job with the Seventh Cavalry."

The rear door to the saloon opened, men spilled into the backyard. Moon glinted on the badge of the sheriff. He and his men spread out and searched the area as Stone and Slipchuck puffed tobacco.

"There they are!" somebody shouted.

Stone rose to his feet, felt pain in his ribs and kidneys due to hard punches in his fight with Benteen. *Even when I win, I lose.* The sheriff approached, followed by a crowd of men. Stone and Slipchuck stood side by side, the top of Slipchuck's hat level with the middle of Stone's chest. The sheriff wore a sandy mustache, crow's-feet at the corners of his eyes.

"Which one of you shot Jess Pollard?" the sheriff asked.

"I did," Stone replied, "and it was self-defense all the way. Anybody who was there'll tell you that."

The sheriff's eyes narrowed suspiciously as he scrutinized the big cowboy. "What's yer name?"

"John Stone."

"You'd better watch yer step in Hays City, John Stone. This is a law-abidin' town, and I ain't afraid of you. You step out of line, I'll lock you up."

A voice in the crowd said, "He cheated me out of my money!"

The poor farmer stood at the edge of the crowd. Slipchuck reached into his pockets. "How much of yer boodle I got, sodbuster?"

"Forty dollars."

Slipchuck placed the coins in the farmer's eager hands. "Go home to yer wife and fambly. Stay the hell out of saloons."

"How 'bout me?" asked the corporal who'd lost an earlier pot.

"And me!" chimed in another loser.

Slipchuck paid them back. The crowd followed the sheriff to the saloon. Stone and Slipchuck sat on the ground. The half moon sat on the horizon like a boat on a choppy sea. Slipchuck flicked an ash on the end of his stogie. "Wish I could be like the other fellers, who rob you with a smile."

Stone always felt wild and strange after a killing. A gypsy fortune-teller in San Antone had predicted he'd die young, and he wondered where he'd be gunned down. He turned to Slipchuck. "Do you remember how we used to get up before dawn when we rode for the Triangle Spur, how good the coffee tasted? I never felt better in my life. Somehow, we've got to get back to that, pard."

Stone missed the cattle drive, but had to go to San Francisco, nearly fifteen hundred miles away across plains and mountains swarming with injuns, because that's where Marie had gone.

"Let's go to the post," he said. "I want to see Custer first thing in the morning and put you on the payroll."

They walked through the alley. Men sat on a bench in front of the saloon, passing a bottle of whiskey. Others stood on the sidewalk, talking loudly. A hush came over them as Stone and Slipchuck appeared. A man thrust his hand at John Stone. "I'd like to say I shook the hand of the galoot what shot Jess Pollard."

Stone walked past him, repelled by the notion. He placed his foot in the stirrup, raised himself onto the back of his horse, a dark brown gelding named Moe, selected by Stone in the Fort Hays stable.

Stone and Slipchuck rode side by side down the street, and the crowd watched silently as they were engulfed by darkness at the edge of town.

Two o'clock in the morning, Stone opened the door of the Fort Hays guardhouse. Private Klappenbach jumped to his feet behind the desk.

"Want to see Antonelli," Stone said.

"Get permission from the guardhouse sergeant."

Stone grabbed him by the front of his shirt. "I said I want to see Antonelli."

Klappenbach picked the iron keyring off the peg and opened the door. Stone entered a small pen in front of the bars, lit the lamp suspended from the ceiling. The pale yellow glow illuminated three men sleeping on the cold dirt floor.

"Antonelli," Stone said softly.

A head popped up, tiny nose, scrawny mustache. Antonelli dragged his ball and chain toward the bars. "Johnny!"

"You're headed for the hospital. Maybe you can get discharged on a medical disability." Stone winked.

Antonelli nodded. The fix was on. It was something a New Yorker could understand. Stone reached into his shirt, pulled out half a loaf of bread and a two-pound chunk of cold roast beef taken from the officers' mess. "Share it with the others."

Antonelli's eyes goggled with pleasure as he accepted the food. "Don't never turn your back on Buford. He's madder'n a wet hen."

Stone reached through the bars and grasped Antonelli's shoulder. "Just hang on awhile longer. You'll be out of here before you know it."

General Custer lay on his back and stared at the ceiling as Libbie cuddled against him. He could feel the rise and fall of her respiration, her curvy body sheathed in a flannel nightgown.

Fort Hays was grinding him down. He was meant for better things. Go east and become a businessman. Run for president. His popularity diminished every day his name was out of the newspapers. But he couldn't leave the Army.

He loved uniforms, parades, guns. Nothing in the world quite like an all-out kick-'em-in-the-ass cavalry charge. The bed confined him, he rolled away from Libbie's warmth, gazed at the moonlit prairie through the window.

Sitting Bull was out there, with Crazy Horse, Gall, and Dull Knife, raiding poor farmers, swooping down on Army patrols, stealing anything that wasn't nailed down. The Kidder Massacre opened Custer's eyes to the truth of injuns. He'd seen soldiers with noses and ears cut off, private parts stuffed into their mouths, long deep gashes everywhere on their bodies, guts spilled onto the ground, filled with arrows. Easterners bewailed the plight of the poor unfortunate injun, but didn't have to live with them.

Injuns were moving toward their winter campsites. By December they'd be low on food, war ponies weak, the ideal time for the Seventh Cavalry to strike, but Washington was afraid to take a stand.

Grant had gone downhill disgracefully since the war. He viewed the presidency as a reward for service to his country, lived like a king while corrupt cronies governed. Washington's a mess, and somebody's got to clean it up.

But he was chained to Fort Hays, a controversial figure, his future cloudy. His reputation would be restored if he could win a great victory against the injuns. He'd led the Michigan Wolverines down Pennsylvania Avenue in Washington during the Grand March after the Rebellion. Feted by one and all, now he was rotting in Kansas, forgotten by a people who'd praised him. He couldn't fade away like other old soldiers. He was only twenty-nine, with the best years of his life ahead.

"Something wrong, Autie?" asked the soft, sleepy voice of his wife.

"Can't sleep. If something doesn't happen soon, I'll lose my mind."

"I won't let you. Come to bed. I'll put you to sleep."

He crawled beneath the covers. She touched her lips to his cheek.

"I don't care where I am, as long as I'm with you, Autie. One day you'll be vindicated, you'll see. There's a time to reap and a time to sow. Be patient. Men like you can never be held back long."

"If only something, anything, would happen," he said.

Private Klappenbach lay asleep on the cot in the guardhouse, when the front door opened. In a second he was upright, gun in hand.

Sergeant Buford closed the door behind him. He locked his rifle in the rack on the wall. The lamp burned dimly on the desk. He glanced at the log. "Anything to report?"

"John Stone was here," Klappenbach replied. "Palavered with Antonelli, who's goin' to the hospital in the mornin'. Then he'll git out on a medical discharge. Son of a bitch spit in an officer's face, and they'll turn him loose."

"Like hell they will!" Sergeant Buford entered the cell block, turned the lamp higher, peered through the iron bars. Antonelli slept near the wall, huddled underneath his blanket.

Buford unlocked the door, charged across the cell block. Antonelli raised his head. Buford grabbed him by the front of his ragged shirt, lifted him off the ground.

"What's this I hear 'bout you gittin' out tomorrow!"

Antonelli wriggled frantically, trying to avoid whatever was coming. "I don't know nuthin' 'bout nuthin'."

Buford slammed him in the mouth. Antonelli dropped to the ground, escaped the kick to his liver, reached for his knife. He bared his ratlike teeth defiantly as the guardhouse sergeant drew his gun.

"You just tried to escape."

Buford's service revolver fired. Antonelli doubled over as if hit in the gut with an ax. Buford aimed at him and squeezed off another round.

Lights went on all over the post. The sergeant of the guard came running. In the barracks, rifle racks were unlocked. The guardhouse filled with armed men, followed by Lieutenant Forrest, new acting provost marshal.

"What's going on here!" demanded Forrest.

"Prisoner tried to escape," Buford replied, sitting calmly behind his desk.

Forrest pushed soldiers out of his way as he made his way to the cell block. Antonelli lay on the ground, clutching his stomach. "How'd he escape?"

"Jumped me."

"Witness?"

"Private Klappenbach."

Lieutenant Forrest turned to Klappenbach.

"It was like the sergeant said," Klappenbach testified.

"Both of you were in this cell, both of you were armed, and the prisoner attacked you?"

"Had a knife." Sergeant Buford handed it to him.

"He took on the two of you with this?"

"Prisoner Antonclli always was a little tetched in the head, sir. It was him or me."

"I want your report on my desk no later than reveille. Carry on."

Lieutenant Forrest left the orderly room. He'd been awake and fully dressed when he'd heard the shot, on his way to a rendezvous with a certain lady. He approached Custer's home, saw the general sitting on his porch, dressed in buckskin pants and jacket, wearing boots. The general had prepared for war at the sound of the first shot. Lieutenant Forrest saluted. "Sergeant Buford shot a prisoner, sir. Says he tried to escape, but I'm not so sure. At any rate, it's all over now. No reason for you to stay awake, sir."

General Custer watched Lieutenant Forrest walk toward the headquarters. The camp became quiet again, lights went out in the barracks. General Custer looked at the sky, an inverted blue bowl covered with diamonds.

It reminded him of the night he'd powwowed with Yellow Robe and Little Bear near the Wichita Mountains. He'd sat in a tipi and smoked the peace pipe, promised never to make war against injuns again, provided everyone upheld the terms of the agreement. The atmosphere was churchlike, and Little Robe told Custer solemnly that if Yellow Hair broke his word, he'd be killed.

The treaty had been violated numerous times on both sides since that night, and the words of Little Robe lay like a curse on Custer's soul. But all a soldier can do is follow orders. A coffin or a medal. Who wants to be an old man?

Stone and Slipchuck peered out the window, looking for injuns creeping among the buildings. Time passed with no more shots.

"Probably some young trooper shootin' at his own shadow," Slipchuck said.

Before them were huts with adjacent tipis. Injun scouts lived in the tipis and used the huts for storage, but most were gone now that no campaigns were under way. Stone and Slipchuck returned to their cots. Stone pulled his blanket over his head. Marie still loved him, that was all that mattered. They'd be together soon, he was sure of it. *I'll find you if it kills me.*

They say a man should be careful what he wishes for, because he's liable to get it.

General Custer entered his dark living room, lit the lamp. He still couldn't sleep, agitated by images of Yellow Robe. He looked at his collection of swords and knives mounted on the wall. His favorite was a prize of war taken from a young Confederate cavalry officer in White Oak Swamp, first man he'd ever killed. Custer pulled it down from the wall. The blade was double-edged, inscribed in Spanish: *No me saques sin razon; no me envaines sin honor.* Draw me not without reason; nor sheathe me without honor. The blade was made of Solingen steel, three inches longer and half an inch wider than the government-issue weapon, hefty and lethal in his fist. General Custer raised it high over his head. Before him stood Yellow Robe, tomahawk in hand. Custer grit his teeth, brought the sword down swiftly.

The Cheyenne chief fell at his feet like all others who dared challenge the Golden Cavalier.

6

STONE ATE BREAKFAST in the Headquarters Company mess hall, a wood-slatted building with rows of long tables lined up on either side of the aisle. The meal consisted of fried hardtack with molasses, bacon, and muffins. The bacon tasted rancid. A baked maggot resided in the muffin. The coffee was thick as mud and evil as Jezebel.

His table was jammed with grumbling sleepy soldiers, some with hangovers, in various stages of uniform regulation. Except for an occasional request for the sugar or salt, they said little.

Stone evaluated them with a professional eye. They'd joined for adventure, or couldn't find work on the outside, and ended at this remote little fort in the middle of nowhere. They had nothing to hope for except discharge, and not much could be expected of them. He dropped his plate at the dishwasher's sink, walked outside, and spotted an officer with the bronze leaf insignia of a major on his shoulder boards.

"Don't I know you?" the major asked.

"We met at West Point, sir. John Stone."

"I'll be damned!" Major Reno took a step backward and looked at the ex-cadet. "It's you, isn't it, Johnny?"

"It's me, all right."

Scheduled to graduate with the class of 1855, Reno didn't get out until 1857, when Stone was a freshman. Reno accumulated 1,032 demerits, a West Point record.

"What're you doing here, Johnny?"

"Hired to scout for the regiment."

"Worked as a scout before? I don't mean to be rude, but the general appoints family and friends to jobs they're not qualified to handle. You and he were quite close at the Point, isn't that so?"

"We were friends, if that's what you mean."

"Unfortunately I wasn't a friend of his, and he treats me like dirt. He's a blowhard and a showpiece, yet he's in command while far better men languish in the lower grades, because they didn't know the right newspaper reporter." Major Reno leaned closer to Stone and narrowed his right eye. "There's a plot to keep me down, and Custer's at the root of it. The man resents me, because I know how stupid and incompetent he really is."

Major Reno paused, a knowing smirk on his face, waiting for Stone to respond, but Stone didn't say a word. He thought Reno was mad, and he was Custer's second in command? How did this lunatic manage to stay in the Army?

"Custer knows how I feel about him," Major Reno said. "I don't care, really. And the feeling is mutual, I assure you. I won't hold it against you, that you're his friend. May we always cherish the happy days we had together when we were cadets at the Point."

Major Reno propelled himself toward the officers' mess, while Stone resumed his walk. How could Custer go into battle with an officer like Major Reno? Stone approached Custer's house, the door opened, General Custer stepped out, wearing his black hat and buckskin suit, dogs yapping at his heels.

"You look a little pale this morning, Johnny. Anything wrong?"

"I just ran into Major Reno."

"He's enough to ruin anybody's day."

"Wouldn't turn my back on him if I were you. Don't depend on him for anything."

"I have to. He's what the Army sent me."

"I've got just the man you're looking for. Do you remember me telling you about a great tracker? He showed up in Hays City, and if you could use another scout, hire him. He can look at the ground and tell you everything that happened for the past week."

"I'll have Sergeant Major Gillespie put him on the payroll."

They arrived at the headquarters building, guards at the door saluted Custer. Sergeant Major Gillespie looked up from his desk as General Custer and John Stone entered the orderly room. "Here's the report on last night's shootin', sir. The prisoner who tried to escape is dead."

"Who was he?"

"Private Antonelli."

The hospital contained two rows of beds separated by the middle aisle. Dr. Shaw directed Stone to a room where Antonelli lay on the table, draped with a white sheet. Stone pulled it away. Antonelli's scrawny frame was marred by two ugly gunshot wounds crying out like angry mouths. The New Yorker's rodent features were frozen in a grimace of pain, his skin was white, Stone covered him with the sheet. *Somebody's going to pay for this.*

He returned to Custer's office. The general sat behind his desk, signing his name to correspondence and documents. "I'm drowning in a sea of paper," Custer muttered, scratching his pen on the bottom of a requisition for ammunition. "I feel like a clerk."

"You've got trouble in your guardhouse," Stone replied. "Antonelli was shot by Sergeant Buford, I'm absolutely sure of it. If a man's trying to escape, how can he get shot in the chest?"

"If you have witnesses, I'll court-martial Buford. What makes you so sure? Maybe the prisoner tried to rush him."

"The prisoner was too smart to rush a man with a gun."

"What kind of vermin spits in his company commander's face? The main problem in this command is lack of discipline. The shooting might send the right message to the garrison: Step out of line, you can be killed."

Stone's anger skyrocketed as he walked out of the orderly room. Nobody cared about the petty criminal from New York City, but Stone had seen his warrior soul. He flung open the guardhouse door. Sergeant Buford looked up from his desk, made a motion toward his gun, so did Stone. Their fingers rested on their handles as they glowered at each other.

"You killed Antonelli," Stone said evenly, "and I'm going to kill you."

"Name the place and I'll be there."

Stone slammed the door in his face. The gunshot corpse of

Antonelli loomed before his eyes. The scrawny denizen of a thousand gutters never had a chance, nobody would cry at his funeral, but somebody would die, that was for damn sure.

Stone arrived at his cabin, threw open the door, Slipchuck sprang up from a dead sleep, aimed his Colt at Stone's head. Stone sat on the bed and worked his jaw muscles.

"What's wrong, pard?"

He told the story of Antonelli's murder as Slipchuck dressed in black britches, yellow shirt, brown cowboy hat.

"Sergeant Buford ain't long fer this world," Slipchuck said, strapping on his gunbelt. "Anythin' fer breakfast?"

"General Custer wants to meet his new scout. Then you can eat, but the food's pretty bad, I warn you."

They walked side by side across the parade ground, tall muscular cowboy and short old man. Slipchuck was nervous, about to meet the great man. Slipchuck read about Custer and seen his picture in newpapers over the years. "What's he like?" Slipchuck asked. "He treat you like a friend, or a shithouse rat?"

"He's still the man I knew at school, only older, wiser, and more disillusioned with life. He's stuck with rotten men and officers, and it's made him glum."

They came to the orderly room. Sergeant Major Gillespie gave them the fisheye as they made their way to General Custer's door. Stone knocked, Custer's voice bade them enter. He sat behind his desk, working through paper.

"This is my pard, Ray Slipchuck," Stone said.

General Custer stared at the bearded old man. A strong wind would blow him away. Could he see anything out of those wrinkled old eyes? "Howdy, Mr. Slipchuck. Johnny here told me you're a great tracker."

"Lived with injuns here and there in me life," Slipchuck replied. "Even had me an injun wife onc't. I knows what the injun knows, and I goes where the injun goes."

General Custer leaned back in his chair. "I know a little about injuns myself. Admire them in a way, but can't tolerate their butchery and lawlessness. One of these days we'll move against them, and maybe you'll be with us."

"Injuns're gittin' mad," Slipchuck told him. "The big tribes ever settle their grudges and come together, you'll have yer hands full, let me tell you."

"They'll never come together," Custer replied. "They've been fighting each other too long, and don't understand modern warfare. The Seventh Cavalry'll ride right through the injun nation, if we ever find them."

Slipchuck doubted the Seventh Cavalry could ride through a Sioux war party, never mind the whole injun nation. He stood uneasily, unaccustomed to the offices of generals, but Stone was at ease. He dropped into a chair in front of Custer's desk, indicated Slipchuck should sit too.

Slipchuck lowered himself, cushions swallowed his bony behind. He crossed his legs and examined the famous war hero at close range.

"Now that I have two good scouts," Custer said, "maybe we ought to organize a buffalo hunt. Why don't both of you see if you can find a herd? Take a detachment with you, in case you run into injuns."

"D'ruther go alone, jest Johnny and me," Slipchuck said. "Soldiers make too dad-gummed much noise."

General Custer pointed his finger at Slipchuck. "You remind me of somebody, and I just realized who it was: my chief of scouts, California Joe."

"That old polecat? Hell, him and me did some trappin' onc't, out in the Rockies. Hell of a good egg. Where's he now?"

"God knows," Custer replied. "Maybe trading with the injuns."

"You ever see him again, you say hello from Ray Slipchuck, got me?"

"I got you," the general said. "What part of the country're you from?"

"I'm like horseshit, I been all over the road."

There was a knock on the door.

"Come in!" shouted General Custer.

The door opened, and Sergeant Major Gillespie stood there, an expression of dismay on his face. "Sir, Major Scanlon's been killed by injuns!"

General Custer's face became alert, his eyes flashed danger.

"They're bringin' him in now. Lieutenant Varnum's patrol found him near the Wakhatchie crossing."

Custer put on his hat, strode out of his office. Stone and Slipchuck followed him to the veranda of the headquarters building. A column of soldiers accompanied by a wagon headed their way, led by a lieutenant with a pointed nose and chin, wearing a forage cap with the crossed swords insignia of the U.S. Cavalry on the front crown.

Custer's lips were set in a grim line. "This country won't be safe until every injun is dead."

The patrol came closer. General Custer descended three stairs to the ground. The lieutenant saluted. "Not pretty to look at, sir."

General Custer moved to the side of the wagon. Major Scanlon lay naked on the floorboards, barely recognizable. Long slashes were on his arms and legs, he was disemboweled, his guts and private parts stuffed into his mouth, nose cut off, eyes gouged out.

General Custer said, "All the tender souls who worry about the so-called plight of the Indians should look at this. There's nothing noble about savages who mutilate and kill."

Slipchuck turned to Lieutenant Varnum. "Any arrows stuck in him?"

"We didn't see any."

"Usually they shoot arrows in, make a man look like a porcupine."

"Maybe they were short on arrows," Lieutenant Varnum said.

"Not fer killin' bluebellies," Slipchuck retorted.

General Custer remembered the Kidder Massacre, arrows protruding from bodies of the victims. "Why didn't they use arrows, Mr. Slipchuck?"

"Maybe they wasn't injuns."

A crowd of officers and enlisted men gathered around the wagon. Stone gazed at the man who slept with Marie until a few weeks ago. "We might find something interesting, we went to where he was killed," Stone said.

"Don't go alone," General Custer replied. "I'll assign a detail to escort you."

Lieutenant Varnum raised his hand. "I volunteer to lead the patrol, sir."

"I'll go too," said a crusty old corporal.

"Don't leave me out," added a young private.

Every man in the vicinity volunteered, surprising Stone. Maybe they weren't such bad soldiers after all.

"We'll go alone," Slipchuck grunted. "You can hear the goddamn cavalry a-comin' twenty miles away."

Stone and Slipchuck headed for the stables. Custer frowned

as he climbed the stairs to the orderly room. If the injuns didn't kill Scanlon, who in hell did?

Private Klappenbach entered the guardhouse just as Sergeant Buford was leaving. "They found Major Scanlon dead near the Wakhatchie River crossing," Klappenbach said. "Sendin' out scouts to check. Don't think it was injuns, cause no arrows was found in Major Scanlon."

"Maybe the injuns ran out of 'em."

"You ever hear of an injun without an arrow?"

"Stay here till I get back."

Sergeant Buford walked across the parade ground, forage cap low over his eyes. John Stone was a troublemaker, but they wouldn't find anything at the Wakhatchie crossing. Sergeant Buford had been careful to hide everything. Maybe one day he'd bushwhack John Stone too.

He arrived at the Company B area, and entered the orderly room. Captain Benteen sat behind the desk in his office, a sheet of paper half filled with writing in front of him.

"What's on your mind?" Benteen asked.

"General Custer was a-gonna let Private Antonelli out of the guardhouse this mornin'. Thought you might want to know that."

"He wouldn't dare!"

"Don't matter now. Antonelli's dead." He winked. "The main thing is who's gonna be the new permanent provost marshal. I think it should be you. The man who runs the guardhouse can do pretty much whatever he wants around here."

Every soldier lived in fear of the guardhouse. Benteen would have an additional instrument of control at his disposal, if he were provost marshal. John Stone could be locked up when Custer wasn't around to protect him, and shot trying to escape, like Antonelli.

"I thought you were one of Custer's boys," Benteen said to Buford.

"A man's got to look out for his own self. You and me can do business, Captain Benteen, that's all I care about."

Libbie sat in her living room, trying to read a book of French grammar, but the wind distracted her. It blew constantly, day and night, no escape from it. She yearned for a silent spot where she wouldn't have to listen, but it was everywhere. Day after day, month after month, wind wailed in her ears.

Sometimes she thought she was losing her mind. She wanted to place the palms of her hands against her ears and scream. Once she tried to hide in the closet, but the wind followed her in. *I've got to calm down.*

Autie needed her, depended on her, loved her. And she loved him. He wasn't the smartest man she ever met, or the most handsome, and certainly not the richest, but he was the most exciting, and that's what she wanted more than anything else.

She wondered if rumors about his dalliances were true. They said he made a squaw pregnant during the Washita Campaign, but Autie swore he was innocent, and Libbie wanted to believe him. The shadow of doubt occasionally crossed her mind. Difficult for a lusty man like her husband to deny himself on a long campaign, with young injun beauties flirting.

The breeze rattled the windowpanes, she lay the book on her lap. If she ever found out Autie had been unfaithful, only one way to pay him back. Maybe handsome young Lieutenant Forrest. John Stone wasn't bad either.

The wind whined over the shingles of the roof. Libbie wanted to bury her head underneath a pillow, but willed herself to remain seated. *I'll get through this somehow. I can't let Autie down.*

Captain Benteen entered the headquarters building and hollered at Sergeant Major Gillespie: "Custer in?"

"At the stable, sir."

Benteen strolled toward the stable, thumbs hooked in his front pockets, twin silver bars of his rank shone on his shoulder boards. If Buford hadn't shot Antonelli, Custer would have let him out of the guardhouse. What worse insult could there be?

West Point fancypants publicity-hungry son of a bitch. Thinks he's better than everybody else. *I been around some generals in my time, but I've never seen such bragging.*

Benteen hated Custer and his entourage. The son of a house painter and storekeeper, Benteen worked his way up from the bottom, fought for everything he had, while Custer arrived with his pretty blond curls, and they handed the world to him.

Benteen considered Custer a fraud perpetrated on the Army by the popular press and sniveling federal government. It was humiliating for an officer of Benteen's experience to take orders from a man five years younger, and so pretentious. Custer strutted around like a peacock, surrounded by ass-kissers and hunting dogs, but this time he'd gone too far.

Benteen balled and unballed his fists as he made his way toward the stable.

On the other side of the fort, Stone walked down Suds Row, where laundresses washed the troopers' clothes. The women lived in wood shacks with chimneys that belched smoke into the sky. The smell of soap and lye was in the air.

He came to a hut with a sign that said EGGLE. He knocked on the door, it was opened by a woman with the long sad face of a horse. She wore an apron and dress wilted by steam and splashes of water. "What can I do fer you?" She pulled a strand of damp hair away from her eyes. On her chin sat a mole with hair growing out of it.

"Hear you do sewing."

"You must be the new scout who knowed old Iron Butt back when."

Stone entered the room. A sturdy table held a washboard and tubful of blue Army clothes. Stone lay his black shirt on the table. "Sew a few bullets into the seam." He dropped bullets onto the shirt.

She drew back her thin lips and showed snaggled teeth. Hair grew out her nostrils. "A man never knows when he might need a few extry bullets, eh, cowboy?" She looked him up and down, and her tiny deep-set eyes took on that special glow. "I got a few minutes."

At first he didn't know what she was talking about, then the awful truth dawned upon him. "My pard's waiting for me. Maybe some other time."

"Won't take long." She winked lasciviously. "Only cost you five dollars."

"Haven't been paid yet."

"How much you got?"

"Couple dollars."

"I'll take 'em, you can gimme the rest payday."

"Got to meet my pard. Sorry." He backed toward the door.

She raised her dress, showed bony knees and skinny thighs. He swallowed hard, opened the door, smiled nervously.

"I knows what you're thinkin'," she said, lowering her dress. "You don't figger I'm so purty, but let me tell you somethin', big boy: After you're in Fort Hays a few more months, you'll come a-crawlin' here on yer hands and knees, but then the price'll be higher."

General Custer strolled though the stable, slapping his riding crop against his boot. He loved to be with horses, the Army had the best, his troopers spent much of their time grooming and taking care of them. The animals stood in their spotless stalls, clean straw on the floor, manes perfectly trimmed, splendid animals.

He looked at a chestnut stallion with black boots, beautiful flowing lines, intelligent eyes. General Custer moved closer to the animal, stroked the animal's forehead and long nose, felt his tremendous power. The big eyes gazed at him calmly. Horses had been shot out from underneath General Custer during the war. They were warriors too.

The stable was General Custer's favorite place. He liked the healthy animal odor arising from the stalls, mixed with the fragrance of hay. In another part of the stable, men groomed the horses. It went on constantly, keeping them healthy and clean for the next campaign.

General Custer heard a footfall behind him. Captain Benteen stood in the middle of the aisle, thumbs hooked in his pockets, deep-chested, agate eyes without expression.

"Just heard a rumor," Benteen said. "You were releasing Antonelli from the guardhouse, although he spit in my face."

"I don't answer to you," General Custer replied. "You answer to me."

Benteen turned down a corner of his mouth. "Same thing happened to Antonelli might happen to you."

General Custer gazed unflinchingly at him. "This is still the Army, Captain Benteen. You threaten me, I'll place you under arrest."

Benteen sneered. "Hide behind regulations, you goddamned coward. I'll take you on anytime, anywhere, name your weapon. You're a liar and everybody knows it. How you ever got to be a general is beyond me."

General Custer quivered from the tension required to keep himself under control. "If you attack me, I'll be obliged to defend myself. So come on."

Benteen wanted to jump all over him, but consequences would be disastrous. Custer was Phil Sheridan's fair-haired boy. Benteen would get the firing squad. "You're brave when troops're around to stop the fight. How's about meeting me at night, when it'll be just the both of us."

"I wouldn't dirty my hands."

General Custer walked away. Benteen stared at his back, tempted to pull his service revolver and shoot him down. The arrogance of the fancy priggish fool with his silly uniforms and giddy wife.

Benteen was white with rage. If he shot Custer in the back, he'd get the firing squad. He withdrew his hand from his holster and closed the flap. Got to be a better way.

Stone and Slipchuck rode past the parade ground, heading for the main gate. Bedrolls were tied behind their saddles, they were loaded with rifle and pistol ammunition, an odd pair with the faraway gaze of desert riders. They passed the sentries at the main gate and rode onto the open prairie, heading for the Wakhatchie River crossing.

"Ain't never liked Army life," Slipchuck said. "Officers a-struttin' like poppycocks with gold braid, while reg'lar soldiers do the dirty work. Closest thing to bein' a slave I ever seen. You ask me, General Custer can take the Seventh Cavalry and shove it up his ass."

Captain Benteen walked across the parade ground. The more he thought about General Custer, the angrier he became. Turned his back on Benteen and walked away. Wouldn't fight a duel. Captain Benteen felt the urge to punch somebody in the mouth.

He angled toward officers' row, so he could have a cup of tea with his poor sick wife. She wasn't holding up well to life in the remote Army post. He wondered what he'd done to get trapped here with General Custer.

A familiar figure appeared around the corner of a building, Major Reno. Benteen resented officers who'd been to West Point, but Major Reno didn't like Custer either, and maybe . . .

Captain Benteen walked toward Major Reno, who shuffled along with his hands clasped behind his back, looking at the ground, mumbling to himself. *He's losing his mind in this damned place,* Benteen thought, *but perhaps I can make use of him.* He drew close to Major Reno, raised his hand in a snappy salute.

Major Reno was drafting a mental letter to the War Department, requesting transfer to a more salubrious installation, when the tall, sturdy figure of Captain Benteen loomed before him. Major Reno returned the salute jerkily.

"I was wondering if I might have a word with you, sir," Captain Benteen said.

Major Reno was surprised. What could Captain Benteen possibly want to say to him? "Go on."

"I'll put my cards on the table," Benteen said. "You don't like Custer and neither do I. Why don't we do something?"

"Such as?"

Captain Benteen glanced around. He wouldn't want witnesses, and would deny everything if he was asked. "You're his second in command, and I'm his third. We're going to campaign against the injuns sooner or later, and you know how Custer pushes everybody to the limits. Maybe you and I won't move so fast one day, or don't do exactly what he wants. Maybe the great general finally'll get what he deserves."

Major Reno was shocked. "Surely you're not suggesting . . ."

Captain Benteen glanced around again, to make sure no one could hear. "Custer could get his ass kicked by the injuns, and if we're lucky, they might even kill him."

Major Reno looked him in the eye. "I ought to report you. This is treachery in the face of the enemy."

"Think over what I told you. We'll talk again."

"But . . ."

Benteen walked away, leaving Major Reno with his mouth hanging open, in the middle of his sentence.

Stone and Slipchuck approached the Wakhatchie River crossing. They could see the trail left by the wagon that carried Major Scanlon's mutilated corpse from the scene, plus the escort of cavalry. As they drew closer to the river, they found an area where wagon wheel tracks were deep and overlapped, the spot where Major Scanlon's body had been loaded aboard.

Stone and Slipchuck dismounted. No blood was on the ground, animals licked away every drop. "What do you see?" Slipchuck asked.

"All these tracks are from shod horses."

"Injuns could be a-ridin' stoled cavalry horses. If you was an injun, what you do with Major Scanlon's duds?"

"Wear them."

"If you wasn't an injun, what you do with 'em?"

"Hide them."

"Let's start a-lookin'." Slipchuck said. "We ain't got all day."

Major Reno sat in his office, drinking a cup of coffee. He had a terrible pain in his groin, his face beaded with sweat.

It was the hernia he'd acquired on the Rappahannock leading a cavalry charge against Fitzhugh Lee. Reno's horse had been shot out from underneath him, and he couldn't throw himself clear. The horse had landed on top of him.

He hadn't been right since. Mail order catalogues advertised trusses and devices to alleviate the pain of hernia, but none worked. His gut protruded from the rip in his stomach wall, producing a bulge the size of a plum beneath his skin. Sometimes it didn't bother him, other times sent shock waves of pain through his body.

He grit his teeth, unable to escape the sharp knifelike sensations. They stayed with him for days sometimes, especially when he did a lot of riding, but he didn't dare complain. If they gave him a medical discharge, what would he do? His wife's family was rich, but they hated him. Everything he'd ever done had gone wrong.

It was galling to take orders from Custer, who'd been a plebe at West Point when Reno was a graduating senior. He was sure Custer held a grudge over the hazing. Why couldn't a horse fall on Custer?

Reno thought of Captain Benteen's proposition. Custer deserved to be defeated by injuns. Show the world what a fraud he was. Divine justice. Major Reno shifted position on the chair, taking the pressure off his hernia.

Maybe they'll give me command of the Seventh Cavalry. My wife's family might respect me at last. The injuns were on their last legs, and anybody could whip them.

Major Reno could see the victory parade, himself riding at the head of the Seventh Cavalry. Maybe he'd wear a unique uniform, like Custer. Sure made a man stand out in the crowd. He and Benteen would wait for the right moment, never do anything might draw suspicion.

Colonel Marcus Reno. He liked the ring of it.

It was late afternoon. Stone rode over the prairie, and all he saw were prairie dog burrows, gopher holes, mesquite, and patches of grass. Moe was surefooted, but not as smart as Tomahawk. Moe had been in the Army too long, didn't think for himself anymore.

A shot! Slipchuck sat atop his horse, waving a rifle. Stone pulled Moe's head around, gave him the spur. Moe plodded toward Slipchuck, and Stone spotted something on the crest of a hill, but it disappeared suddenly. Were his eyes playing tricks on him?

Injuns saw you before you saw them. That was the law of the West. They might be watching him and Slipchuck, ready to spring the trap. Stone removed his Colt from its holster and pulled alongside Slipchuck. On the ground, a hole four feet deep surrounded by tracks. Stone dismounted, examined the sign.

"What you see?" Slipchuck asked.

Stone's brow furrowed with thought. He took out his bag of tobacco and rolled a cigarette. Then he roamed about on his hands and knees like a dog, eyes close to the ground.

"It's starin' you right in the goddamned face," Slipchuck said.

Stone rose to his feet and pointed back to the Wakhatchie River crossing. "Major Scanlon was killed back there by a white man who wanted to make it look like the injuns did it. He stripped Major Scanlon and mutilated him, but couldn't leave his weapons and uniform lying around. He rode over here and buried them."

"That hole looks empty to me," Slipchuck said.

"That's because the killer didn't know injuns were watching him. After he left, they dug up the uniform and equipment, because injuns don't let anything go to waste."

Slipchuck climbed down from Buckshot, and extended his hand. "You figgered it out. Ain't much more I can teach you. You know pretty much what I do."

They shook hands, the torch of knowledge passing.

It was midnight in Hays City, and Sergeant Buford strolled past the hog pens, smoking a cigarette. His eyes were half-closed, he'd already hit several saloons, now wanted some loving.

The walk was narrow, lined with small shacks. Whores stood in the doorways, and when a soldier came close, they opened their robes and showed what they had.

"Hey, Sergeant, let's have us some fun."

Buford passed her silently. He liked them with more meat on their bones. Bead curtains and crimson bedspreads could be seen through windows. A whore turned around, bent over, picked up her dress. Buford stopped in his tracks. Now there was a woman.

She faced him, opened her bodice. Her breasts were low-hanging, plump blond in her mid-forties, face hard as a man's.

"How's about it?" she said.

"Don't mind if I do."

He followed her. Someone plunked a banjo in the street. They entered her shack. She undressed, no preliminaries, he didn't care, took off his clothes, hung them over a chair, placed his gun on the little table near the bed.

"What you want that fer?" she asked, stepping out of her pantaloons.

"Like to have it close by."

"I was guardhouse sergeant, I'd watch my ass too."

She knew who he was, a man of important position. She pulled back the covers and crawled into bed.

"Let's git it over with," she said. "I ain't got all night."

He crawled onto her soft body, buried his head between her breasts, saw a thin white scar across her throat from ear to ear.

"Anything wrong?" she asked, noticing his sudden change of mood.

It looked as though somebody tried to kill her. "Injuns do that?"

She lowered her chin, folds of fat covered the scar. "It was a soldier boy like you. Liked to cut on women. You here for a conversation, or you want to fuck?"

She was a tough one, but pretty for Hays City. He hugged her. It didn't take long. The whore rolled out of bed and washed herself. "This ain't no hotel room for the night."

"I know what it is. Not the first time I rutted with hogs."

She was accustomed to insults. Long as they paid their money and kept knives out of sight, she didn't care what went down. He donned his uniform, tied his yellow bandanna around his neck.

He didn't want to leave her, but couldn't afford more.

He walked outside, and headed toward the Tumbleweed Saloon. A woman's raucous laughter erupted behind him. Two young soldiers approached on the sidewalk.

"Howdy, Sergeant Buford," they said in unison.

Everybody wanted to stay on the good side of the guardhouse sergeant, and they'd better. He ever caught them in the guardhouse, they'd wish they were never born. He placed his hands in his pockets and passed darkened storefronts closed for the night. Ahead, shafts of light angled into the street from the windows of saloons.

"Buford!"

The guardhouse sergeant turned at the entrance to an alley, and saw the silhouette of a man at the other end. "Who's there?"

"Come in and find out."

The voice sounded familiar. Something told Buford to get the hell out of there, but instead he advanced into the alley. "Show yer goddamn face, you son of a bitch!"

John Stone stepped into the moonlight. "They'll court-martial you someday, Buford, but I can't wait that long." He reached toward his boot, and pulled out his Sioux knife.

Buford smiled. "I been a-hopin' to see you again. I'm a-gonna hang yer hide on my wall."

Buford drew a knife from the scabbard on his belt. Both men dropped into crouches, but there wasn't much room in the alley. They could advance or retreat, no circling. Stone got low, holding the Sioux knife before him, the balance felt right. His fingers pressed on the turtle, horse, eagle, and lobo. Buford advanced, probing with his blade, his free arm out for balance.

Stone watched carefully. In the dark, a man with fast hands could kill you before you knew what happened. Stone thrust his knife forward, but Buford was waiting. He caught the wrist of Stone's knife hand, pulled him closer, and drove his blade toward Stone's guts.

Stone's forearm whacked Buford's knife to the side. Both men crashed into each other, then pulled back. Buford slashed at Stone's belly. Stone raised his hand to protect himself, but Buford cut Stone's forearm to the bone. Stone pulled back, warm liquid trickling down his fingers. The parameters of the fight suddenly changed. Stone had to finish Buford before too much blood was lost.

Buford spat contemptuously. "Want to knife fight me? I *invented* knife fights. Try that again, I'll cut yer head off, and throw it in the gutter."

The odds were with Buford now. If he held Stone at bay, Stone would fall at his feet. "C'mon," Buford said, beckoning with his free hand. "A little closer."

Blood spurted out the cut on Stone's arm. Buford planted his feet firmly on the ground, bent his knees. "I'll cut you from hell to breakfast." He pushed his knife forward, free hand floating in the air.

Stone rushed him, head down. Buford took a step to the side, but the wall prevented him from dodging farther.

Stone sidestepped to cut him off, Buford took a swipe at Stone's head, Stone ducked and thrust his knife toward Buford's midsection. Buford lowered his arm in time, Stone's blade slipped into Buford's forearm muscle.

Buford shrieked as Stone's knife ripped meat like a chef boning the drumstick of a turkey. Buford crashed into the wall, bounced off, attacked Stone's throat. Stone leaned back while Buford's forward motion brought him closer. Stone's knife plowed a jagged red furrow across Buford's nose and cheek, nearly severed his ear from his head.

Buford went mad with pain, screaming at the top of his lungs. On the backswing, Stone ripped his blade across Buford's chest, then buried it to the hilt in Buford's belly.

Buford's eyes protruded in horror, hairlip grotesque, Stone's hand awash with warm blood. He brought his face close to Buford's and twisted the knife. "That's for Antonelli," Stone said. Buford moaned, blood tinged his lips. Stone turned the knife again. "That's for me."

Buford's legs gave way. Stone took a step backward and held the bloody Sioux knife in the air. Slipchuck's voice came to him from the back of the alley. "Let's git out of here, pard."

It was two o'clock in the morning. General Custer paced back and forth in his darkened living room, slapping his riding crop against his leg. He was furious with himself for backing down before Captain Benteen. West Point indoctrination had done it to him. A commanding officer doesn't brawl with subordinates.

What was his breaking point? He wanted to take his trusty old saber down from the wall, and chop Benteen's head off.

But he was General Custer. His courage and fighting prowess had been demonstrated many times. He had nothing to prove. It took all of Custer's much-vaunted willpower to hold himself back. *What an ugly evil-looking monster. I'll can't let him get away with it.*

He lit the lantern on the table, turned to the wall, pulled down his trusty old cavalry saber. He could see headlines in newspapers across the country:

CUSTER DECAPITATES OFFICER
IN ANGRY FRONTIER DUEL

Let them write what they wanted. Nobody insulted Autie Custer and got away with it. He'd hack the son of a bitch to death. He drew the sword from its scabbard.

"Autie?" Libbie at the top of the stairs, wrapped in her frowsy wool robe, looked down at him. "Where do you think you're going?"

He gazed at the weapon grasped tightly in his hand. He'd actually been on his way to chop Captain Benteen's head off! He smiled unsteadily. "I . . . ah . . . couldn't sleep."

"Neither can I. The wind . . . oh, Autie, I hate this place."

He dropped onto a chair. "I'm losing my mind. If you hadn't stopped me . . ."

She knelt beside him, lay her cheek against his leg. "I don't know what to do anymore."

"Maybe I should leave the Army."

"When the next Indian campaign begins, you'll want to be in the thick of it. I know you too well. You could never be an ordinary man."

He'd sit at a desk on Wall Street, and grow a potbelly. The dashing young cavalry commander would disappear. "Maybe I should put in for a transfer."

"And leave the Seventh Cavalry?"

The Seventh was his own personal honor guard and striking force, held together by the strength of his will. But he couldn't handle Fort Hays much longer.

"Maybe you could get a furlough," she said. "We'll go to New York, and by the time we return, Washington will make up its mind about what to do about the Indians. I don't think General Sheridan would turn you down, after all you've done for him. I'll write the letter."

Libbie had a way with words, Little Phil liked her, the many advantages of a pretty wife. "Sounds fine to me."

She took his hand. "Come to bed."

He followed her up the stairs. She made everything sound so simple. They crawled into bed, giving each other solace in the cold Kansas night.

A solitary light shone in the dining room of another house on officers' row. Captain Benteen sat at the table, maps spread out in front of him. He was studying the Washita Campaign of 1867.

An officer's fighting style was a clue to his personality. At the Washita, Custer divided his men into four components that attacked from four different directions. It violated a basic rule of warfare, never split your forces in enemy territory, but Custer was a gambler. It was more important to confuse the enemy, the better to roll over him.

Benteen leaned back in his chair and puffed his corncob pipe. Coordination was everything in a multipronged attack. If one or two units failed to reach their objective, the odds would turn against Custer. He never let anybody get in front of him during an attack, and once he got in among the injuns, he wouldn't last a minute. Then the world would know at last that Custer's luck was hot air.

It was better than killing Custer outright, because defeat would hurt more. Benteen yearned for the day Custer would be disgraced. He'd do his best to bring it about, now that he'd opened lines of communication with Reno.

Most men pray for peace and prosperity, but Captain Benteen wanted war. Time the world found out the truth about the Boy General. *You think you're smart, but I'll show you. Your name will be mud, when I'm finished with you.*

Stone opened his eyes. The sting in his forearm prodded him to consciousness. Thick clouds blocked the moon and stars. Slipchuck snored peacefully on the other side of the clearing.

The bleeding had stopped. He'd come through another fight in one piece, but how long could he keep it up? He picked up the Sioux knife and looked at the carvings on the handle. So strange, in the alley, he'd felt like an injun, crazy mind-rattling experience. His new knife had been christened with blood.

Stone lay the knife beside him. He was tired, but a few days of rest and buffalo steaks would rebuild his strength. His forearm throbbed, his mind blended with the pain as he drifted into the twilight world.

Above him floated the head of a grinning coyote, blood dripping from its fangs.

7

General Custer stood at attention, breeze lifting his long blond mustaches. His command was assembled on the cemetery ground, paying their final respects to the guardhouse sergeant, lying in his coffin beside an open grave.

The chaplain intoned theological platitudes, while General Custer worried that recent events at Fort Hays might draw the attention of the War Department. Captain Benteen beamed hatred at him, and Major Reno acted even more peculiar than usual. Libbie was a nervous wreck, though she kept it well hidden, and Custer was ready to draw his saber on Benteen. Custer still wondered whether he did the right thing when he walked away from the commander of Company B in the stable.

The bugler played taps, the guardhouse sergeant sank into his cold dark grave. Nobody cried, the troopers hated and feared him, he came to rest in the bottom of the hole. The bugler reached the end of taps. Custer gave the order to dismiss the men. The command was passed down, the formation broke apart. Custer walked toward his house, hearing shovels of dirt falling onto his former guardhouse sergeant.

Two riders entered through the front gate, Custer recognized John Stone and Ray Slipchuck returning from the buffalo reconnaissance. He remembered the last hunt of the season, his spirits rose.

"Found your buffalo, General." Stone pointed toward the southwest. "Big herd with plenty of grass. Probably won't go anywhere for a while."

"What happened to your arm?"

"Fell down. By the way, injuns didn't kill Major Scanlon." Stone told Custer what he and Slipchuck had discovered at the Wakhatchie River crossing. "Had to be a white man."

"Wonder who it was?"

"He have any enemies?"

"Worst enemy was himself, except maybe the . . ."

"The what?" Stone asked.

"Guardhouse sergeant. We just buried him this morning. Knifed in Hays City. When the soldiers aren't fighting injuns, they fight each other. The guardhouse sergeant was no friend of yours, I don't suppose."

"Hell no," Stone replied, not able to look his friend in the eye.

"Let the sawbones have a look at your arm. We'll go after the buffalo first thing in the morning. You've done good work. Take the rest of the day off."

Dr. Shaw sat at his desk, reading a book. He was in his fifties, with salt-and-pepper hair. "What can I do for you?"

"Had an accident." Stone sat at the desk, untied the bandage. The wound was three inches long and bone deep.

"Looks like it's healing all right," Dr. Shaw said. "Best let Mother Nature take its course, but I'll put on a fresh bandage. How'd you get it?"

Stone had the answer prepared in advance. "Fell on a nail sticking up out of a floorboard."

"Looks like a knife wound. You hear what happened to the guardhouse sergeant?"

Stone nodded.

"I imagine he got a few licks in on whoever killed him, but that's none of my business. You're the gentleman who went to West Point with the general?"

"A long time ago," Stone replied.

"Somebody told me you knew Marie Scanlon. Helluva nice person. She was a patient of mine."

"What was wrong with her?"

"A cold, a pain, women's troubles, all the usual symptoms. Boredom more than anything else. That's our biggest problem here. She's not the first person driven to desperation by day after day of nothing to do."

"You ever meet Canfield?"

The doctor affixed the dressing to Stone's wound. "He was a patient of mine too."

"What'd he have?"

"Lung disease."

"Serious?"

"Probably, but he was an interesting fellow. I can understand why Marie liked him. Marvelous sense of humor, could quote long passages of Shakespeare extemporaneously. Seemed to know about everything. Been in the war."

"Somebody told me he knew Marie before the war."

The doctor shrugged. "They certainly got along well. Some people on this post don't have anything good to say about Marie Scanlon, but I thought she was a fine woman, and she always played fair and square with me. Many's the afternoon we sat in this very office, talking about whatever came into our minds. Her opinions on Army life had me rolling on the floor. I'm sorry about what happened to the major, but I don't believe people ruin other people. We ruin ourselves. If Marie Scanlon walked through that door right now, I'd be happy to see her."

Stone entered the sutler's store. Slipchuck sat at the table against the far wall, with a few troopers. Two officers sat at another table. Stone made his way to the bar.

"What's yer pleasure?" the sutler asked Stone.

"You got anything that doesn't have alcohol in it, like sarsaparilla?"

"Sarsaparilla!" exploded the trooper next to Stone. Stone recognized him: Lieutenant Forrest's supply sergeant. "Can't be a man, you drink that pisswater."

Stone looked at the sutler. "I said sarsaparilla."

"Don't got none. No root beer or ginger beer either. I can offer you a cup of coffee."

"If it's not too much trouble."

"Not too much trouble?" the supply sergeant asked. "What kind of man's afraid of whiskey? Are you a girl?" The supply sergeant pushed Stone contemptuously. "Get the hell away from me."

Stone didn't budge. The sutler placed the mug of coffee on the bar. Stone reached for it, but the supply sergeant whacked the mug into Stone's belly, covering his new shirt with a dark stain. A fist flew at Stone's face a second later. He leaned to the side, the punch whistled past his cheek. The supply sergeant grinned, showing a missing front tooth. His nose had a dent in its side, his features lumpy, veteran of many a barroom brawl, but you can't let a man throw coffee at you and get away with it.

Stone stepped away from the bar. The supply sergeant followed him, his fists raised high, protecting his face peekaboo style. Stone carried his own fists low, to lure him in. The supply sergeant pawed with his right hand, measuring Stone for the straight right, but Stone was a veteran of many a barroom brawl too.

The supply sergeant snapped his left fist at Stone's forehead, and Stone jerked to the side, opening himself wider. The supply sergeant unleashed his big straight right, and Stone was waiting. He blocked the punch with his left arm, and threw a right hook to the supply sergeant's head.

It connected, and the supply sergeant heard bells clanging. He blacked out for a second, and when his vision cleared, he was shocked to see a fist streaking toward his nose. He couldn't run, no place to hide. The fist connected, the supply sergeant was lifted off his feet. He crashed through the front window and flew through the air. Two passing troopers watched in astonishment as the supply sergeant landed a few feet away.

Stone made his way toward the door, the bandage on his left arm soaked with blood. Frustration, mix-ups, failures, and defeats welled up in him like boiling acid. The supply sergeant dragged himself to his feet, saw three John Stones in front of him. He raised his hands to protect his shattered nose, and Stone's fist rammed into his belly. The wind went out of the supply sergeant, he struggled to breathe, Stone bashed him again. The few bones still intact inside his nose were demolished, and the supply sergeant felt as if he'd run into a house. Tripping and sprawling backward, struggling to stay upright, Stone worked his midsection with short chopping punches. Again the supply sergeant was forced to lower his guard. Stone threw a hard left hook at his head. The supply sergeant was thrown to the ground. When he landed, he didn't move. Stone returned to the sutler's store, leaned his belly against the bar. "Another cup of coffee."

The sutler reached for the pot. Slipchuck approached the bar. "You better git that wing looked at by the sawbones."

"I want a cup of coffee."

The sutler placed the mug on the bar. Stone raised it to his lips, feeling the wanton madness of fighting. He gulped the hot black liquid, it steadied him, but what he really needed was whiskey.

He had to stay away from the stuff. His left arm was going numb, he raised it into the air, blood soaked his shirt. Slipchuck led him out of the sutler's store. A crowd gathered around the supply sergeant. Stone grit his teeth against the pain in his arm.

He couldn't understand why people didn't leave him alone. He never bothered anybody. At least one madman in every saloon. He and Slipchuck arrived at the hospital. Dr. Shaw arose behind his desk. "What'd you fall on this time?"

Slipchcuck aimed tobacco juice at the spittoon beside the desk, wiped his lips with the back of his hand. "He just beat the shit out of the supply sergeant of Company D."

"That so?" Dr. Shaw asked. "He's Jimmy Fitch, the heavyweight boxing champion of Fort Hays."

Slipchuck slapped Stone on the back. "This is one tough son of a bitch."

The doctor unwrapped the wound, sopped the blood with a white cloth that quickly turned bright crimson. "Maybe we should stitch it up."

"Whatever you say," Stone replied. "Just don't cut anything off."

The doctor took a bottle of whiskey out of his medicine cabinet. "You'd better have some of this."

Stone stared at the whiskey. He hadn't had a drink for two weeks, and didn't want to start now. "Think I'll try it without the whiskey," he said.

The doctor held up the needle. "It'll take about ten stitches. We'll have to tie you down."

"All right with me."

"Whiskey makes it go easier."

"I'm not a drinking man."

"Got some laudanum, but folks say it's worse than whiskey."

"Nothing's worse than whiskey."

The doctor poured some into a glass, topped it off with water, handed it to Stone, who tossed it down in one gulp. It had a tart chemical taste, no kick at all. "Sure you gave me enough?"

"Have a seat, while I prepare."

The door opened, and a group of soldiers carried the supply sergeant into the office. Still out cold, he was laid on a bed. The doctor bent over the supply sergeant and pulled back his eyelids. "What you hit him with?"

Stone rolled a cigarette with one hand, licked the paper, popped it into his mouth. Slipchuck lit a match and held it in the air. The doctor puttered around on the top of his medicine chest, passing the needle through the flame of a candle. The soldiers who accompanied the supply sergeant looked at Stone, and he stared at them maliciously.

They made for the door. The doctor chuckled as he threaded the needle. Stone looked at his wound oozing blood. He leaned forward, Slipchuck held out his hand. The last thing Stone saw was the needle gleaming in the candlelight.

Stone woke up with a headache and a sore arm. Slipchuck sat beside his bed, cleaning his Colt. They were in their shack at the edge of Fort Hays; it was growing dark. Stone raised his arm, saw the clean white bandage. He placed his feet on the floor, was assailed by dizziness.

"You all right?" Slipchuck asked.

Stone reached into his shirt pocket, took out his bag of tobacco. His shirt was torn, he remembered the one he'd left with the seamstress. "Be right back."

He reached for the doorknob, missed it the first time.

"Want me to go with you?" Slipchuck asked.

Stone walked outside. The sun sank behind the stable, streaks of red and gold covered the sky. On the parade ground, the bugler blew tattoo, a guard detail lowered the flag. Stone made his way to Suds Row. The laudanum hadn't left his system yet. Not bad stuff.

The pain hadn't bothered him when the doctor sewed his arm. The Comanches could attack Fort Hays, he wouldn't care. What was the use of worrying? He felt light-headed and free. The world wasn't such a bad place after all. So what if he was on a remote post in the middle of nowhere, no money in his pocket, his girlfriend run off with a gambler. A man had to count his blessings.

He came to Miss Eggle's cottage, knocked on the door. Her eyes lit up when she saw him.

"If it ain't the new heavyweight champeen of Fort Hays."

"My shirt ready?"

She pulled it off a peg, held out the lower hem. "Here's yer bullets."

They felt like smooth pebbles between his fingers. He removed his torn shirt, handed it to her. "Think you can fix this, and sew a few bullets in the hem like the other one?"

"Anything you say." She moved between him and the door. "There's somethin' I want to ask you." A naughty twinkle was in her eye.

"I've lost some blood," he replied, putting on the clean shirt. "And I'm engaged to be married."

She placed soap and water-reddened hands on his chest. "I've taken a shine to you." She smiled, teeth green and black, cheeks ravaged by acne, eyes bright with desire.

"Got to go home."

He leaned against her, she got out of the way, he nearly fell.

"You're a fool," she said. "All you care about is what you see, but things that count most ain't on the outside. You and me could have a business. Fortunes bein' made by folks with brains, but the fools with pretty faces, you know where they end up?"

There was a knock on the door. Miss Eggle reached behind her and turned the knob. A young private stood at attention. "General Custer wants to see Mr. Stone at his residence, sir."

Stone turned to Miss Eggle. "Pick up my shirt tomorrow?"

"Think over what I told you."

Stone followed the young private out of Miss Eggle's cottage. Night coming on, sky stained with purple, lanterns burning in windows. Stone felt floaty and strange. The buildings were made of rubber, undulating in the night breeze. Did he love Marie just for her pretty face? What was beauty anyway? To the poor lonely soldiers at Fort Hays, Miss Eggle was the belle of the ball.

Stone and the soldier approached Custer's house, sounds of merriment issued from within. The soldier opened the door.

"Who's there?" shouted Custer.

John Stone walked toward the voice, came upon men and women seated at a table, platters of food before them.

"May I present the new heavyweight champion of Fort Hays!" General Custer said.

The assembly applauded. Custer sat at the head of the table. "Have a seat, Johnny. Help yourself."

The fragrance of food rose to Stone's nostrils. He realized he was famished. Someone passed him a platter covered with thick slices of meat. Custer held out a bowl of boiled potatoes in butter sauce. Stone tried to remember his South Carolina table manners as he filled his plate. The woman to his right poured water in his glass. He checked her profile, in her late teens. Across the table sat a lovely woman in her mid-thirties. Last night he'd slept beneath the stars, now dined with officers and beautiful females; it reminded him of the old days.

General Custer introduced Stone to his guests, names flew over his head. The only person who made an impression was the general's kid brother, Tom Custer, with the same sharp nose and eyes as Fannie, wearing the gold bars of a second lieutenant on his shoulder boards.

"You must be a tough fellow, to knock out Sergeant Fitch," Tom said. "He's still in the hospital. You broke his jaw."

There was silence. Stone had no idea of what to say. He looked down and saw himself sitting at the table, reaching for his utensils.

General Custer cleared his throat. "Thought we might organize an exhibition of boxing here. Our best men against the champions from Fort Dodge. Sergeant Muldoon of that installation is the present heavyweight champion of the Seventh Cavalry. We could put together an attractive purse. A hundred dollars to the winner."

Stone woke up suddenly. If he had a hundred dollars he could leave for San Francisco *immediately.* "Who's Muldoon?"

"A veteran of my old Michigan Wolverines. Don't enter into this lightly, Johnny. He's knocked out all his opponents so far, including Sergeant Fitch, the man you put into the hospital."

"How long did Fitch stay in with him?"

"Nearly twenty rounds, wasn't it?"

Captain Myles Moylan, sitting on the opposite side of the table, said, "Eighteen, I believe."

Stone knocked Fitch out in a few minutes. But Fitch had been drunk. "Let me think it over."

"Wouldn't want to rush you. Muldoon is an awfully rough fellow. I can understand your caution."

Libbie Custer interjected, "Stop it, Autie. You're trying to goad him on. Muldoon is a terror. Boxing isn't entertainment."

"You could be disfigured for life," said the young woman to Stone's right. "Didn't Muldoon thumb out somebody's eye once?"

Custer said, "Nobody'd think the less of you if you don't fight him, Johnny. He's dangerous, no question about it. I thought you might be able to use the money, and you whipped Fitch. He was a first-class fighting man himself."

"I have a better idea," Libbie said. "Why don't we do a play? Something from Shakespeare. *Macbeth,* or *Julius Caesar.*"

"My wife wants to bring culture to the frontier. Unfortunately, the men aren't interested. They'd rather see a good fight. Think it over, Johnny. Let me know when you make up your mind."

Stone sliced his steak. Best to follow Marie soon as possible, while her trail was hot. A hundred dollars could do it. Travel by train. In a week, San Francisco.

"Johnny?"

Stone looked at General Custer. All eyes were on him. Had he done something wrong?

"You went away from us for a moment there," General Custer said. "You all right? I was telling you about the buffalo hunt, but you weren't listening. You sure Fitch didn't hit you harder than you thought?"

"My grandmother hit me harder than Fitch."

"Maybe we can sweeten the pot to more than a hundred dollars."

Stone's ears perked up. Most of his fights had been for nothing except the cuts and bruises he had when it was over. A hundred dollars was three months pay to a cowboy.

"Tell me about Muldoon," he said.

"Couple inches taller than you, maybe fifty pounds more. A few years older. Nobody's stood up to him before. Keeps coming at his opponents and wears them down."

"Brute force, mostly," added Lieutenant Varnum. "A man who knows how to box could beat him. Do you know how to box, Captain Stone?"

"A little."

"Afraid you'll need more than a little."

"Saw him fight once at Fort Dodge," Captain Yates said. "Man's got a head like a block of granite. Took punches that would've stopped another man in his tracks, but he kept on." The officer smiled at John Stone. "Give it some thought. Don't be dazzled by money. A man like Bull Muldoon hits you in the right spot, he could kill you."

At the far end of the table, Libbie frowned. They were all gentlemen until they talked about violence. Then a strange maniacal sheen came over their faces, they became ogres, her husband most of all.

"I saw him fight once at Fort Dodge too," the Boy General said. "If I had to face him, I'd take a cannon into the ring. Only thing to stop Bull Muldoon."

Stone reached for the salt, his arm brushed that of the lady to his right, their eyes met. He glanced away quickly, shook some salt on his potatoes. He felt her knee against his, then it moved away. Their eyes struck sparks again. He didn't remember her name.

"We were all surprised to learn," the woman said, "that you knew Marie Scanlon, and you were supposed to marry her?"

"That's still my intention," he said. "Were you a friend of hers?"

"Marie Scanlon and I didn't hit it off too well. I'm from Vermont, and she didn't cotton to Yankees."

"Unless," said another woman, whose name Stone also couldn't remember, "you happened to be a high-ranking officer. Then she could be quite gracious. She certainly ruined Major Scanlon, and probably was responsible for his death."

Eliza served cake and coffee. Stone's left arm throbbed with pain. Injuns could heal it in a few days with plants. They knew more about medicine than white doctors who graduated from famous colleges, but you couldn't ride to the nearest injun village for a consultation. They'd kill you before you got close, but your wound wouldn't bother you anymore.

After the meal, the men retired to the parlor for cigars. The walls were covered with trophies, citations, swords, the heads of dead animals staring down balefully through imitation glass eyes. Stone slipped out the back door. It was pitch-black except for a fire burning beneath a caldron of bones and fat in a thick malodorous porridge that reminded him of supper in the guardhouse. Stone wrinkled his nose as he moved into the darkness.

On the prairie, he longed for a town. When in town, he wanted the prairie. He never felt comfortable anywhere, a strange discomfort prodded him continually. But he'd been happy with Marie. Something about the way she talked and moved, and she told strange mysterious stories. If he held her in his arms again, he could do anything.

He heard a sound behind him, General Custer leaving the house. "Don't shoot, Johnny. I'm not an injun."

Stone pointed the barrel of his gun at the caldron. "That what you feed the prisoners?"

"It's what I give my dogs."

"Could swear it's what we ate in the guardhouse."

General Custer was hatless, hair thinning on top of his head, cigar in hand. "I've been thinking, Johnny. If I recommended you for a commission, General Sheridan would give his approval. I could use you here. You'd be a captain before long."

Stone shrugged. "Don't think so."

"You're just saddle-bumming around. You'd have a future, an outlet for your talents."

"My scalp would end up on the belt of a Cheyenne warrior."

"Happens to civilians more often than soldiers. What other alternative do you have? Can't be a vagabond all your life."

"I want to have my own ranch in Texas someday. I like to work outdoors with cattle and horses. When I came up the trail with the Triangle Spur, I was never so happy in my life. Hate to spend the rest of my days on this Army post with Reno and Benteen."

"If only I could replace Reno with you."

"If Major Reno were my commanding officer, I'd go over the hill. How can you rely on him?"

"A lot of good men like yourself don't want any part of the Army."

"No sense of duty, you probably think."

"As a matter of fact, that's exactly what I think."

"Let somebody else lead the next charge."

"You were on the losing side. It's made you bitter, I'm afraid."

"Stop playing soldier and come to Texas with me. I know cattle, and you know rich folks in New York. We could put a ranch together. I tell you, it's the greatest life in the world."

"Unless injuns pay you a social call. Then you'll get down on your knees and pray for the timely arrival of men like me who play soldier. The life of a rancher isn't for me, Johnny. Wouldn't want to spend the rest of my life playing nursemaid to a bunch of dumb cows."

"Longhorns cost six dollars in San Antone, but four times that in Kansas. You have a few thousand head—add it up."

"Mathematics was never my strong suit."

"A profit in the neighborhood of forty-five thousand dollars a year, not counting your expenses, which maybe come to half that. I'd say that's pretty good money."

"When I was in New York, I met men who earned a million dollars in a year."

"What good does it do them? I'd rather be in the open air, on a good horse, with my friends."

"New Yorkers live quite luxuriously. They have everything they want, including the finest restaurants in the world. The women are truly amazing. Each is more beautiful than the last. They wear their dresses down to here." He placed the edge of his palm against his chest. "You can see Christmas and a little bit of New Year's."

"You're a married man. Better forget about Christmas and New Year's."

"I was thinking about you."

"Sure you were."

They laughed. The back door opened, and Libbie Custer appeared. "What's so funny?"

"We were talking about New York," General Custer said.

She approached, hugging the shawl around her shoulders. General Custer placed his arm around her.

"I've been trying to convince Johnny to join the Seventh Cavalry," Custer said.

"Why would anyone in his right mind want to do that?"

Stone replied, "To save America from the injuns, but who's going to save the injuns from America?"

"The injun is an extinct species," Custer said, "but he doesn't know it yet."

"He knows it, but he's not giving up without a fight."

"He wants a fight—the Seventh Cavalry will make short work of him."

"Are you talking about the same Seventh Cavalry that you said was the dregs of humanity?"

"They fought for me at the Washita, they'll fight for me again."

Libbie said, "Did the both of you argue like this at West Point?"

"Isn't it strange," Custer replied, "that I, who graduated last in my class, with tons of demerits, was the first to make general, while this man, who won high marks in everything, is working for me?"

Stone poked his forefinger into Custer's chest. "You made general because you were a great soldier. That has nothing to do with grades at West Point. Look at Wade Hampton. The man never studied one page of military strategy in his life, and became the best cavalry commander we had. It's a quality you have inside, and nobody could ever take it away from you."

"You have it too, but don't want to use it."

"All I want is a ranch in Texas. Spit and polish isn't my game."

"When injuns raid your stock, you'll run to the nearest Army post."

The door behind them opened, the woman who'd sat next to Stone appeared. "Thought I'd get some fresh air."

Libbie shivered. "Getting too fresh for me. Think I'll go inside."

General Custer accompanied his wife to the door. As he passed the woman, he caught a whiff of rose perfume. *So that's her.* She was full-bodied, pretty, dark hair. Stone still couldn't remember her name. Was she wearing a wedding ring?

"Looks like rain," she said with a frown. "Buffalo hunt'll be postponed." Her perfume wafted over him. They stood in silence for several seconds. "I hope you don't intend to fight that Muldoon fellow."

"I've pretty well made up my mind to do it."

"Surely you're not *that* desperate for money."

"I don't have a penny to my name, and I'm in debt to the general for the clothes on my back."

"There must be another way to earn a hundred dollars. Aren't they paying you for whatever you do around here?"

"I can earn more in one night than if I worked as a scout for three months."

"What if you get hurt?"

"I can take care of myself."

"I don't think you understand. They're just *using* you. They don't care whether you get blinded or disfigured. It's just another diversion to keep them from thinking about their boring stupid lives. If you get killed, they'll bury you beside Major Scanlon, and next day they'll go on a buffalo hunt. That's the kind of people they are, and your Marie was worse than all of them."

"I don't mean to be rude," Stone said, "but who are you?"

"I'm a friend of Annie Yates. We went to school together back east. My name's Jane Hemphill."

"Sounds like you didn't like Marie very much."

"A little flirt, beneath her fine southern manners. You're throwing your life away on her. You want a hundred dollars? I'll give it to you. You needn't pay me back. Don't fight for money. You're too good for that sort of thing."

"What makes you think so?"

She looked into his eyes. "Don't fish for compliments."

"A man can always use a few compliments."

"You won't get them from me. I'm bored too. That's why I came to Kansas, but it's worse than Burlington. I want to do something with my life, but can't do it alone. I need a man, but so far all I've found are tin soldiers."

"What would you do with the man when you find him."

She gazed at him steadily. "Everything."

He was about to invite her back to his shack when the face of Marie loomed before him. His feet shuffled nervously. She waited for him to say something. If Marie could sleep with Major Scanlon, Lieutenant Forrest, and Derek Canfield, why couldn't he run off with Jane Hemphill?

"I guess you don't like me," she said.

"Until my wedding's off, I've got to . . ."

"Idiot!" she said vehemently.

She marched back to the house. Opportunities constantly came his way. One man wanted to make him a banker. Another offered him half a town. He could've married a beautiful woman who owned a ranch near San Antone, and a man couldn't ask for more. A lady with a big restaurant wanted him to be her fancy man, nothing wrong with that. *What's this outmoded moth-eaten code that I live by?*

His worst fear was one day he'd be old and poor like Slipchuck, regretting the years he wasted in his futile search for Marie. But the search might be over soon. He'd hop the first train to San Francisco. All he had to do was defeat Bull Muldoon.

He knew how to beat a fighter who came straight at you. *Give him side-to-side movement, pick your shots, wear him down. Don't ever go toe to toe with him, stay off the ropes, and don't get caught with anything. California, here I come.*

8

THE HUNTING PARTY left Fort Hays at six o'clock in the morning, ladies bundled in coats and sweaters, a bright red scarf wrapped around General Custer's neck. A detachment of cavalry and a wagon filled with supplies accompanied them. Some of the officers were in high spirits, the kind that flows from the mouths of bottles, and they sang "The Girl I Left Behind Me" as if going on a real campaign against wild injuns.

Stone and Slipchuck, a mile ahead, led the way to the killing ground. The sun shone brightly, the breeze cut into Stone's jacket. *Should be easy to find Derek Canfield in San Francisco. Just hit all the gambling joints.*

"Injuns," Slipchuck said.

Stone's snapped back to Kansas. "Where?"

Slipchuck pointed. "To the right of the notch."

"I don't see anything."

"He came up, took a look, ducked down."

Stone glanced back at the shooting party. Thirty soldiers in the detachment should be able to handle any war party that might turn up. They were hunting buffalo, but were injuns hunting them?

"Johnny," said Slipchuck, "I been a-thinkin' about the big fight you're a-gonna have with Muldoon. They say you can clobber him over the head with a sledgehammer, he won't go down, and when he hits you, he breaks ribs. The odds is a-runnin' agin' you five to one, and there ain't many takers. Maybe you should back out while you got the chance. Jest say yer arm ain't good enough."

"I can beat him," Stone said. "Got him figured out. Wish I had some money to bet."

"How can you figger him out if you ain't never met 'im? I thought when you got sober, you'd be smarter."

They spotted the buffalo herd in the distance, a vast dark brown blanket extending to the horizon. Stone pulled back his reins and brought Moe to a stop. He pulled the Army spyglass out of his Army saddlebags. A big bull stared at him, working his jaws, his head grotesquely huge, pointed beard on his chin.

"There that injun again," Slipchuck said. "Lookin' fer news, I reckon."

Stone gazed at the unceasing prairie. He couldn't blame land-hungry white men for coming here. It appeared uninhabited, but was home to injuns whose way of life had no place for ranchers and farmers. Stone hoped he'd be somewhere else when the big fight came.

He climbed down from his saddle, loosened the cinch, rolled a cigarette. The hunting party arrived. General Custer pulled out his spyglass and looked at the buffalo. "Meat for the winter."

He took command as if planning a military campaign. The hunters would approach the herd from upwind. The detachment, commanded by Lieutenant Forrest, would remain with the women. General Custer kissed Libbie good-bye.

The officers and scouts rode toward the herd, Stone in front with General Custer. "I tell you, Johnny," Custer said, "it's wonderful to get away from that fort. Out here in the open air—that's where I belong."

The herd drew closer, peacefully munching grass. A few animals watched the hunters with dull blinking eyes. Stone had hunted buffalo with a long-distance rifle. You shot one, the buffalo beside it chewed grass as if nothing happened. Death had no reality for them. You could shoot buffalo all day, the rest of the herd would ignore increasing numbers of brothers and sisters getting hit all around them.

Custer pulled his ivory-handled pistol, rolled the cylinder, checked his loads. They reached the edge of the herd, and buffalo stared at them blankly. Custer drew back the hammer of his revolver, and kicked his horse's flanks.

The horse leapt toward the buffalo, and the officers followed, guns drawn. The hunt was on! Slipchuck rode among them, wind whistling through his beard, but Stone stayed back, leaning on his pommel, watching.

The hunters charged into the midst of the buffalo, firing their pistols. Buffalo in the vicinity stampeded, while only a short distance away, other buffalo continued their leisurely meal.

General Custer leaned to the side, fired his gun behind the left front shoulder of a racing buffalo. The immense animal lowered his head, his legs lost coordination, he hit the ground and did a somersault. Custer shouted victoriously.

Slipchuck rode low in his saddle like an injun, fired a shot into a big bull buffalo, the creature crashed into the grass. Nearby, Tom Custer aimed his pistol at a buffalo, hit his head, the bullet didn't even faze the animal.

Stone sat cross-legged on the ground, puffing a cigarette. Dead buffalo dotted the ground, as hunters continued the rampage, killing wantonly. They cheered, urged each other on, and the buffalo seemed not to know what to do. If buffalo had intelligence, they could mass and trample the riders to death.

Stone thought he saw something several hundred yards to his right. When the sun shone on the prairie, he often saw dots and strange moving objects that disappeared. Hard to know what's real out here.

What would injuns think of the spectacle before them? They used every ounce of the buffalo for tipis, clothing, food, sewing needles, waterbags, bedclothes. It was an economic loss for injuns whenever a white man killed a buffalo. Travelers shot buffalo out the windows of trains. Professional hunters slaughtered them by the thousands for their hides.

The number of dead buffalo increased, as officers rode among them, firing guns. Buffalo hunting was good training for war, except the buffalo couldn't fire back. The hunt continued until late in the afternoon, and the prairie was carpeted with corpses. At four o'clock, Custer fired three rapid shots into the air, signaling the end of the hunt. The officers dismounted, cut tongues out of the animals, added them to see who shot the most.

The outcome wasn't a surprise, Custer the winner. A few of the animals were butchered, meat loaded onto the wagon. The rest were left for lobos, buzzards, and rats.

Custer rode toward Stone. "Don't like hunting buffalo?"

"Not in the mood," replied Stone, back in the saddle again.

"Great sport," Custer said, his face radiant. "Not as easy as it looks. One wrong move, a buffalo could gore a man." The smile on his face vanished as he stared over Stone's shoulder. Stone turned, an injun war party appeared out of a ravine behind him. They were led by a chief wearing a long warbonnet of eagle feathers. Custer stuttered in astonishment; Stone pulled his new Army carbine out of its scabbard. Officers and hunters in the vicinity hopped on their horses and rode toward Stone and Custer.

Custer looked at the detachment guarding his wife and the other women. It was a lethal situation, the women needed the detachment more than he. He looked at the approaching injuns, and wondered if Wounded Bear's prophecy was about to come true. He raised his arm in a gesture of peace.

Stone didn't trust injuns who carried rifles and lances and wore garish war paint. The wind rustled the feathers in their hair. They stopped one hundred yards away, then the chief in the warbonnet and two warriors left the assembly and rode toward them.

"Must've recognized me," Custer said. "Wish I had an intepreter."

"I speak some injun," Slipchuck said.

"Johnny, you want to come with us?"

Tom Custer prodded his horse forward. "Take me, Autie."

"Don't leave me behind," said Captain Moylan.

"Me either," added Lieutenant Varnum.

"Three of them," Custer replied, "and three of us. The rest of you stay put."

Custer, Stone, and Slipchuck rode toward the hostiles as officers watched with worried expressions. In the distance, the detachment formed a skirmish line in front of the women.

"I don't think we have anything to worry about," General Custer said confidently. "I'm well known among them, and their chief evidently wants to pay his respects. We'll exchange compliments, it'll be all over. If they want to massacre us, would've done it by now."

"They're wearin' war paint," Slipchuck replied. "Either they're goin' out on a raid or just comin' in from one."

"They fight among each other all the time," Custer told him. "They're a warlike people, but there's something magnificent in their culture."

The three injuns came closer, hands empty except for reins. The chief sat erectly, bareback on his war pony, red and black war paint on his face and body.

"I'll move ahead to meet them," Custer said. "I want to show them I'm not afraid. If it's anything an injun can't tolerate, it's a coward."

Custer prodded his horse, raised his right hand in the air, showed an open palm. His horse plodded forward, Custer alone with three injuns. He smiled, revealing white teeth. "How."

The chief and his two cohorts ignored him, riding toward John Stone. Custer's eyebrows knitted together, he turned to see what the hell was going on. Stone gazed at the chief smeared with war paint.

"Today you have clothes that fit you, John Stone," said the chief. "I almost did not recognize you."

It was Black Wing. They stared into each other's eyes. Custer rode toward them, mystification on his face. "You know each other?" he asked incredulously.

"We've met," Stone said. He rode forward, extended his hand. Black Wing shook it.

"Wondered what happened to you," Black Wing said. "Thought you died."

"I don't die easy."

"Everyone dies easy, you shoot them in the right place."

General Custer cleared his throat. Usually he was the center of attention at conferences with injuns. "How do you know each other?"

"John Stone is a very brave man," Black Wing said. "He is also a very funny man." He looked at Stone. "You ever find the thief who robbed you?"

"Not yet."

"So now you work for the bluebellies. That is too bad." Black Wing looked at the dead buffalo. Stone detected a flash of anger on Black Wing's face. "The buffalo you killed would feed a tribe for a winter," Black Wing said.

"Take them," General Custer said graciously. "They're yours."

"We have other business today."

No one wanted to ask what it was. General Custer smiled. Black Wing turned to John Stone. "Why don't you come with us?"

Stone felt strangely tempted. Break out of his world and put on war paint, live in a tipi far from the corruption of civilization.

"Maybe another time," Stone said.

"Still the woman?"

Stone nodded.

"Bring her with you. A warrior needs his woman."

"I haven't found her yet."

"You are a strange man, John Stone. Your medicine is very strong. I feel it here." Black Wing slapped his stomach.

The horizon called out to Stone. He could live like an injun, dance around bonfires all night, to hell with jobs and newspapers. "I promise you, one day I'll accept your invitation."

"I will look forward to our next meeting, John Stone."

Black Wing turned to Custer. "Yellow Hair, you should leave this place, otherwise you will surely die like the buffalo you have killed this day."

"I . . ." Custer said, intending to make a major policy statement, one he could send his friends who worked for newspapers—*Custer Stands Up to Indians*—but Black Wing rode away. Custer felt shunted aside. The injun had been more interested in John Stone.

Custer twisted in his saddle and looked at his old friend. This wasn't the fellow he'd known at West Point, or was it? "Where'd you meet him, Johnny?"

" 'Bout ten miles from here."

"Did you fight with him?"

"He just laughed at me."

Slipchuck stroked his beard. "Gents," he said, "we almost just got killed, whether you realize it or not."

"Nonsense," General Custer replied. "They wouldn't dare."

"They had nothin' to lose."

General Custer furrowed his brow. A major war party. "Wonder what they're up to?"

"You'll find out a'fore long," Slipchuck replied.

General Custer watched the injuns receding into the distance, and felt a strange premonition. "Load the wagon and let's get out of here," he ordered. "The hunt is over."

9

THE DAY OF the big fight drew closer, as anticipation grew among units of the far-flung Seventh Cavalry. Betting was light at first, and nobody gave John Stone a chance.

Then forces of the free market came into play, odds climbed slowly. At seven to one, there were few takers, but when the scale tipped at ten to one, action heated up.

Soldiers discussed the fight in the barracks, on patrol, at the sutler's store, in the saloons of Hays City. The big question was, how long would it take Bull Muldoon to knock out John Stone.

A new avenue of betting opened at payday stakes. The fight would end in the first round, many soldiers wagered. A few bet on the second and third rounds. No one thought it would go past five. According to the rules, the winner would be determined when one fighter was knocked out, with no designated last round.

A ring was erected on the prairie near the barracks, with hemp rope and long posts driven into the soil. Chairs would be brought from the mess hall for ladies and officers.

Every morning John Stone ran two hours around Fort Hays. He punched an old mattress nailed to the side of his shack another two hours. He ran in the afternoon, then spent the rest of the day fighting the mattress.

He was the object of great curiosity in the mess hall where he took his meals. He went to bed early, awoke before reveille, led a disciplined life although his inclination was to become a wild Indian.

Slipchuck was his manager, trainer, second, and cut man, providing Stone with the benefit of his many years of experience.

"I remember onc't when I was a young feller, got in a fight in a stagecoach stop out New Mexico way. Son of a bitch had a knife in one hand, broken bottle in t'other. I kicked 'im in the balls—he caved in like a concertina."

Stone punched the mattress as General Custer approached, followed by dogs. It was the first time they'd seen each other since the buffalo hunt.

"How's our new champion coming along?" Custer asked. "I bet fifty dollars you'd win, so don't let me down."

Stone was shirtless, pounding the mattress, working toward maximum power at the point of impact. "Do my best."

"Funny thing how it snowballs. We'll have quite a crowd. Most people don't think you'll get past the first round."

Stone didn't have time for palaver. He had to be a fighting machine, no emotions, without mercy. Beat the shit out of him, take the money and run.

General Custer puffed his cheroot thoughtfully. Stone had put on weight since he was in West Point, but not around the waist. Muscles rippled every time he threw a punch, his torso decorated with old knife and saber cuts, plus a few bullet holes and a gash probably caused by a jagged edge of canister. The man had seen much fighting, but so had Custer. However, Custer hadn't been wounded beyond a scratch or nick, and never spent a day in a field hospital. It made him feel invincible.

Custer thought he was intruding. People generally deferred to the Boy General, but not John Stone, who punched his mattress as though Custer didn't exist. "C'mon," he said softly to his dogs as he headed back to his office. "Let the man train in peace."

Captain Benteen watched John Stone from the window of his orderly room. He could rest his rifle on the sill, and squeeze off a round, a powerful temptation.

Muldoon would do his work for him. Benteen had seen Muldoon fight several times in the past. The man was devastating. John Stone couldn't stand up to him. No one else ever had. Muldoon's knee never touched the ground in his boxing career. He was unbeatable.

Benteen wagered fifty dollars against fools who believed in miracles. The white-haired officer with marshmallow eyes couldn't wait for the fight to begin. Bust him up, Muldoon. Split his head open.

Slipchuck entered the sutler's store for his afternoon glass of whiskey. He stepped up to the bar, and the sutler placed the brew in front of him. Slipchuck tossed a few coins onto the bar.

"How's yer fighter comin'?" the sutler asked.

"Real fine," Slipchuck replied. He glanced behind him, the sutler's store was empty, he sat on a chair and propped his boots on the table.

The sutler watched with shrewd eyes flashing dollar signs. "How long you think he'll last?"

Slipchuck took a deep breath and said stentoriously, "My fighter will win by knockout in the sixth round."

"You can't be serious!"

"You don't know John Stone. I seen him take on a whole saloon onc't, and when it was over, he was the onliest man standin'."

"I don't doubt," said the sutler, "the man knows how to brawl. But Muldoon eats saloon fighters for breakfast. I don't think you understand. After Muldoon wins a fight, his opponent generally goes to the hospital."

"Like I said, you don't know John Stone."

"Wanna bet?"

"Already placed my bets," said Slipchuck, and it was true; he'd put five dollars on John Stone's fists, no point going overboard.

"You had faith in yer fighter, seems though you'd bet more. How's about fifteen to one? You talk a good game, but you don't back it. If the fighter's own manager don't believe in him, how in hell's he a-gonna win?"

Slipchuck reached into his pocket, took out his money. Only eighteen dollars left. He dropped it on the bar. "This is all I got in the world. You cover it at fifteen to one?"

"Goddamn right I do," said the sutler as the snare snapped shut.

• • •

Muldoon arrived the afternoon before the fight, with a contingent of officers and men from Fort Dodge. He rode in an ambulance, they couldn't let anything happen to their champion.

A crowd gathered around the vehicle, peering through windows at the best fighter in the regiment. On the fluffy cushions sat a gigantic man with a battered face and crooked nose, huge mangled ears.

The ambulance stopped near the ring, the door opened by a short, potbellied corporal. Bull Muldoon stepped to the ground, and soldiers cheered. He raised his arm in acknowledgment.

Stone heard the applause, but couldn't let himself be distracted. He punched the mattress, his fists a steady tattoo. Sweat poured from his torso, stained the waistband of his britches. Every blow sent a shock wave across his arm and through his body. He grit his teeth and banged away. *I have to win.*

That night at Fort Hays the regimental band provided music for a dance in the mess hall. Soldiers danced with each other due to the shortage of women, drank punch spiked with whiskey, and tried to forget their miserable barren lives.

The sound of their merriment could be heard on officers' row, where General Custer and Libbie sat in their office, writing. The general's topic was the Indian problem, an article he'd send to newspaper friends in the East.

On the other side of the desk, Libbie stared at the blank sheet of paper before her. Her journal contained ongoing impressions of life at Fort Hays, and there was an element she thought should be included.

She didn't know how to word it. She had no difficulty with buffalo hunts, weddings, and birthday parties, and even made an oblique reference to Lieutenant Classen's drumming out, but never commented on the strange sexual tensions at a remote Army post.

It was frightening and titillating to be a woman among so many men. She felt their eyes on her wherever she went. No one dared say a word, fear of the guardhouse holding them back, but a man can be brazen with his eyes, undressing a woman shamelessly, ravishing her brutally. She shivered in her chair.

Some of the soldiers were extremely handsome. The repressed lust of men without women was a palpable force she could feel.

No record of Army life would be complete without mention of it, but what could she say?

If Autie read it, no matter how carefully she couched the words, he'd go through the roof. Keep it light and breezy, dear. Don't look for trouble.

It was a chilly night, and John Stone sat on the prairie a few hundred yards from the encampment. He wore his fringed buckskin jacket, hat low over his eyes. No insects could be heard, winter was coming, formations of geese and ducks flew south all day.

He looked at the sky radiant with stars. Tomorrow was the big fight, and a man's body a fragile envelope. No telling what might happen. Muldoon had sent his last five opponents to the hospital.

The fight would be over this time tomorrow. He'd be on the way to San Francisco, or with Dr. Shaw. A big advantage if he could get a good night's sleep. The man who weakened first would go down.

He approached his shack, saw movement in the shadows, hand dived to his gun. A familiar voice laughed softly, General Custer emerged into the moonlight.

"Thought I'd stop by to wish you well," he said. "Didn't want to do it in front of the men, because the commanding officer can't show favoritism. I've now got a total of a hundred dollars riding on you, so you know who I'll be rooting for." He held out his hand. "You're a helluva guy, Johnny. Good luck."

Slipchuck lay on his bunk, reading a newspaper as Stone entered the shack. Slipchuck glanced at Stone out of the corners of his eyes as Stone prepared for bed.

"Feelin' jumpy?" Slipchuck asked.

"A little."

"Somethin' wrong with you if you didn't. I been in some fights myself, and I know. If'n it goes against you tomorrow, and you're takin' a beatin', just lay down, and let the referee count you out. Don't kill yerself fer a hundred dollars, ain't no point bein' a dead hero, understand?"

10

SERGEANT MAJOR GILLESPIE STOOD in the middle of the ring, attired in a recently laundered and neatly pressed blue uniform, his boots shining brightly in the sun. "And now, ladies and gentlemen! The main attraction of the afternoon! For the heavyweight championship of the Seventh Cavalry!"

A cheer arose from the crowd, as far off on the prairie, animals and birds turned their heads. It was a cloudless day, cool but not cold. Stone stood in his corner, a towel over his shoulders, shifting his weight from one foot to the other. Slipchuck's hand was beneath the towel, massaging the muscles in Stone's back.

"I'd like to introduce at this time," said Sergeant Major Gillespie, "representin' the garrison at Fort Hays, the challenger, our acting chief scout—*John Stone!*"

Scattered shouts of approval erupted from the small number of intrepid souls who'd bucked the odds and placed money on John Stone.

"And in this corner, representin' the garrison at Fort Dodge, the Heavyweight Champeen of the Seventh Cavalry, the great Bull Muldoon!"

Hats flew into the air, men hollered wildly. Muldoon was a massive hulking creature covered with thick slabs of muscle, while Stone was almost puny compared with him. *Here goes a hundred dollars,* Custer thought.

Sergeant Major Gillespie motioned for the fighters to join

him in the center of the ring. They advanced, Stone working his shoulders and dancing lightly on the balls of his feet, Muldoon solid and steady, a confident and friendly smile on his face. When they were only a few feet away, Muldoon winked. "Don't worry, darlin'. I won't hurt you too bad."

Stone didn't reply. Lowering his gaze, he listened to Sergeant Major Gillespie's fight instructions.

"No thumbs, no bitin', no punches below the belt. If you knock yer man down, go to a neutral corner and wait till I call you out. If I tell you to break, I want you to step back. Shake hands, let's give the boys a good fight."

Stone returned to his corner, Slipchuck pulled the towel off his shoulders. Across the ring, Muldoon punched the air. The mess sergeant hit a ladle against an old cow bell. The fight was on.

The friendly smile vanished from Muldoon's face as he advanced in a straight line across the ring. Stone held his hands high and danced to the side. Muldoon veered to cut him off, and Stone darted in the other direction. Muldoon found himself facing thin air.

"Stand still and fight!" somebody shouted at Stone. The crowd booed. Muldoon turned, saw Stone on the other side of the ring.

"What's the matter, darlin'? Wish you was someplace else?"

Stone danced to the side, keeping his hands high. He studied Muldoon's posture, looked for quirks, bad habits, possible openings. Would Muldoon lower his right hand when he threw the left? Muldoon stalked him confidently. Soldiers hooted their disapproval. "Stop runnin', you goddamned coward!"

If Stone wanted the title, he had to take it away from Muldoon. He danced closer, measured distances. Muldoon threw a thunderous hook to Stone's left kidney, but Stone caught the blow on his elbow. Muldoon hooked Stone's right kidney, Stone blocked it with his forearm, took a step backward, got set. Muldoon advanced, Stone threw an uppercut. Muldoon leaned backward, it whistled harmlessly past his nose.

"You'll have to do better'n that, darlin'," Muldoon said.

Stone drove his fist into Muldoon's belly, it felt as though he'd punched a brick wall. Muldoon ignored the blow as he slammed a jab at Stone's face. Stone blocked it with his free hand, hurled a hard right to Muldoon's nose, Muldoon dodged and slammed Stone in the ribs.

The wind went out of Stone for a moment, he tried to get away. Muldoon elbowed him into the ropes, a roar of expectation arose from the crowd. Slipchuck screamed, "Get out of there!"

Stone tried to dodge, but Muldoon muscled him, butted him with his head, punched his right kidney, left kidney, caught him with an uppercut, while Stone's arms flailed helplessly.

He pulled himself together, hunkered into a defensive pose, threw a flurry of body punches. They didn't faze Muldoon, who took a step back and measured him for the knockout punch. Stone slid across the ropes, spun out, and suddenly was behind Muldoon. As Muldoon turned around, a hard-driving fist smashed into his nose. Stone followed with a crunching blow to Muldoon's jaw, then hit him with an uppercut.

Muldoon appeared unaffected as he stepped forward and threw a straight right. Stone brushed it aside and danced away, aghast. He'd hit Muldoon with the best he had, and nothing happened.

Stone danced around the ring, flicking out jabs, as Muldoon tried to corner him, a fiendish grin on his face. He feinted a lunge at Stone, who dodged to the right, but Muldoon anticipated the evasion, and threw a terrific left hook to Stone's side. Stone thought his rib cage was busted for all time, the pain made him squinch his eyes, he lowered his elbow to protect the sensitive area, and Muldoon followed with a hook to Stone's wide-open head.

Stone's legs turned to rubber. He jumped on Muldoon, and tried to hang on, but Muldoon muscled him away, and threw a sharp uppercut. Stone's head snapped back, and Muldoon slammed him in the gut. Stone tried to protect his vital midsection, but a big black shadow covered his face.

He had no idea where he was. Sergeant Major Gillespie hollered: "Five!" Stone opened his eyes, the sound of a waterfall in his ears. "Six!" Stone struggled to get to his knees as Muldoon raised both his fists in victory.

Saved by the cowbell before the count of ten, Stone wondered what world he was in. Slipchuck jumped through the ropes, carrying a bucket of water. He threw it in Stone's face, and a flock of birds migrated through Stone's head. Slipchuck grabbed Stone's arm and dragged him to the corner.

Slipchuck dabbed a rag at the two-inch cut on Stone's forehead. "Stay away from him this round." He handed Stone a tin cup full of water; Stone rinsed his mouth, spit into a bucket, thc liquid tinged red. "You're a-fightin' his fight," Slipchuck said. "You should be a-fightin' yer fight."

Stone gazed across the ring at Muldoon, whose back was being rubbed by his second. A big smile was on Muldoon's face, his manager evidently congratulating him on a great first round. Stone was a proud man being humiliated. The monster in the opposite corner had to feel pain like any other human being. *If I keep punching, he'll fall.*

The bell rang, but Stone didn't come out dancing. He moved flat-footed to the center of the ring.

"Still here, darlin'?" asked Muldoon, a strange mocking smile on his face. He pawed at Stone's face with his left fist, and measured him for a knockout punch, but Stone slipped to the left, coming around and hammering Muldoon in the kidney, then dancing back sharply, avoiding the left jab counterpunch that eddied the air at the tip of his nose.

He threw a hook under Muldoon's left jab, landing on Muldoon's other kidney, then took a step to the side, and jabbed Muldoon in the face. Stone then felt a punch in his ribs, whacked Muldoon in the face, Muldoon elbowed him, spun him around, and put him against the ropes.

Stone covered frantically as Muldoon slammed his body and head. The crowd screamed for blood. Stone's head was knocked back, smashed again and again. He fought back gamely, looking for openings, driving jabs through, his punches had no effect on Muldoon. *What do I have to do!* Muldoon smashed Stone's left forearm, and Stone felt a throb from his knife wound. Muldoon leaned in and butted Stone's head again.

Blood flowed into Stone's eye, he raised his hand to protect the wound, when Sergeant Major Gillespie jumped between them. "Step back!" he ordered.

Muldoon retreated a few steps, and Sergeant Major Gillespie looked at the cut above Stone's eye. "It's a bad one. You want to keep on?"

"Get out of my way."

Sergeant Major Gillespie retreated, and Muldoon charged in for the kill. Stone danced backward toward the center of the ring. He was dazed, recalling Slipchuck's advice about lying down. But he needed that hundred dollars.

Muldoon advanced after him, pawing with his left hand,

trying to set Stone up, while Stone plotted tactics. Muldoon appeared impervious to his punches, and had a head like a rock.

Muldoon lunged, and Stone threw a quick hard, short jab, catching Muldoon coming in. Muldoon appeared surprised more than hurt, and threw his punch, but Stone wasn't there. Muldoon turned around, and Stone danced in front of him.

Muldoon threw a jab, but Stone beat him to the punch, knocking Muldoon's head back. Muldoon hooked Stone to the ribs, but Stone danced away.

If I beat him to the punch each time, I can win this fight. Stone danced on his toes, holding his fists high. Vision in his right eye was tinged with red, his body ached from Muldoon's hard punches. He had to outspeed Muldoon.

Muldoon advanced sideways, presenting a difficult target to Stone, who lowered his right hand, inviting Muldoon in. Muldoon saw the opening, feinted toward it, and Stone threw his Sunday punch, realizing with a sickening sensation that Muldoon had tricked him.

Muldoon's fist crashed into Stone's face, and Stone staggered. Muldoon rushed forward, and Stone timed him coming in, but his rhythm was off. Muldoon hammered Stone's body and arms, then threw one over the top.

"Three!" said Sergeant Major Gillespie.

Stone opened his eyes. He lay flat on the ground, blood dribbling from his mouth.

"Four!"

Stone rolled over, got to his knees.

"Five!"

He rose unsteadily, and Muldoon was in front of him, a mean, glint in his eyes. He threw a punch at Stone's gut, Stone blocked it, and fired a shot at Muldoon's head. It connected, but Muldoon was unfazed as he slammed Stone in the left eye.

Stone went flying against the ropes, bounced off, and Muldoon was waiting for him. Both fighters threw punches at the same time, both punches landed, Muldoon was unmoved, but Stone was thrown to the ground.

The bell rang. Slipchuck ran toward Stone with another bucket of cold water, and dumped it over his head. In the officers' section, Libbie leaned toward General Custer. "Can't you stop it?"

General Custer shook his head.

"It keeps on like this," she said, "he may be injured for life."

"He can give up if he wants to."

Slipchuck helped Stone to the corner, and Stone dropped onto the stool. He sipped water as Slipchuck dabbed blood from his face. The cut over his eye widened, his lower lip was broken, head full of muddy water. Now he could see why Muldoon never was off his feet in the ring. But Stone couldn't throw in the towel. *I've got to hurt him.* He conjured the most sensitive parts of the human body: nose, pit of the stomach, kidneys, eyes.

The bell rang, and Stone jumped to his feet. Muldoon ran eagerly across the ring, but Stone tried to dance away. His legs wouldn't follow orders, and Muldoon collided with him before Stone got three steps out of his corner.

"Six!"

Stone rose to his feet. He stood, Sergeant Major Gillespie moved in front of him. "You all right?"

Stone nodded. Sergeant Major Gillespie stepped back, Muldoon waded in, and Stone dived on him, smothering his punches, trying to clear his head. Muldoon tried to break loose, but Stone wouldn't let him go. They waltzed around the ring as the crowd jeered.

"Step back!" ordered Sergeant Major Gillespie. Stone refused. Sergeant Major Gillespie tried to pry them apart. "You don't let him go, I'll disqualify you."

Stone took a step back. The ground didn't tilt beneath his feet anymore, he'd recovered for the time being. Muldoon rushed forward, and Stone shot a left jab to Muldoon's nose, then darted out of the way of Muldoon's counterpunch. A trickle of blood appeared at the corner of Muldoon's nose, he smeared it with the back of his hand, the mocking smile vanished from his face.

Encouraged by the damage, Stone went up on his toes and danced, his hands held high. He felt normal except for a persistent high-pitched whine in his left ear. Muldoon came after him, snapped out a jab, but Stone leaned to the side and avoided it. Muldoon fired a shot at Stone's left kidney, but Stone let fly a right jab to Muldoon's nose.

Like an enraged monster, Muldoon came forward, throwing punches from all angles. Stone stepped back and to the side.

Muldoon found himself facing a ring post. The crowd burst into laughter at the expression of surprise on Muldoon's face.

Muldoon turned around, and received a punch in the mouth. But he didn't even blink. With an angry growl he charged, throwing a left jab. Stone leaned to the side, launched an uppercut, and Muldoon's head jerked back. Stone drove his fist into Muldoon's midsection, and Muldoon blew air out the corner of his mouth as he wrapped his big hairy arms around Stone, spun him against the ropes, and pounded his body.

Stone dug in his heels, clenched his teeth, and punched back. This time he wasn't going to slide away. He had to make Muldoon respect him. They stood in the corner ripping punches. Stone felt terrible blows rain upon him, but held his ground and responded with everything he had. He landed heavy shots on Muldoon's head and shoulders, bashed his kidneys, rattled his liver, but Muldoon wouldn't step back.

Stone tasted blood on his lips, his right eye nearly closed, and didn't know where he was for moments at a time, but his fists never stopped flying.

The bell rang, Stone staggered to his corner, and the crowd applauded him for the first time. Collapsing onto the stool, he wore a dizzy grin. "I can win this fight."

Slipchuck sopped blood on Stone's face with a wet towel. The cut over his eye was an ugly red cavern all the way to the bone. Stone spat blood into the bucket. Slipchuck couldn't stanch the blood from Stone's eye. "Johnny, I think it's time to throw in the towel."

"One more round."

The bell rang, and Stone arose from his stool. Muldoon advanced across the ring, his nose stuffed with cotton to hold back blood. Stone decided to slug it out with him, what the hell. They came together in the middle of the ring and cut loose.

Stone blocked most of Muldoon's blows on his shoulders and arms as he bore in, aimed careful shots, and kept his chin down. Muldoon feinted with his left, Stone moved to block it, and got hammered with a straight right. The sun went into full eclipse.

"Five!"

Stone opened his eyes, and a cricket chirped in his right ear.

"Six!"

He pitched to his feet, his head crashed against a ringpost, and he turned around. Muldoon was in front of him, and Stone tried to step to the side, but his legs wouldn't move. Muldoon got low and dug his fists into Stone's body, forced Stone to lower his guard, and then shot a jab to Stone's jaw.

Stone's head flew backward; he thought it detached from his shoulders. He ducked, dodged, dived on Muldoon, and hung on. Muldoon head-butted him again, wrestled Stone loose, and threw an uppercut on the inside.

"One!"

Stone raised his head. A trooper bent toward him and said, "You cain't fight to save yer ass!"

"Two!"

Stone got to his feet, tried to dance, but his knees were jelly and his feet numb. Libbie Custer covered her eyes as Muldoon advanced for the last time. Stone wiped the blood from his left eye and tried to focus on his adversary. A towel flew into the ring.

"That's it!" said Slipchuck.

"Like hell it is!" Stone roared. He stumbled forward, and kicked the towel through the ropes.

Sergeant Major Gillespie moved in front of Stone. "What's it goin' to be?"

"The fight isn't over yet."

Sergeant Major Gillespie brought his hands together, indicating the war should go on. Stone hid his face behind his fists, waiting for Muldoon to come closer. Muldoon closed the distance quickly, and threw a straight left at Stone's head. Stone ducked underneath it and tackled Muldoon around the waist, twisting hard. Muldoon lost his balance, they fell against the ropes, broke through the opening, and landed on the ground outside the ring.

The bell went off. Stone disentangled himself from Muldoon and both fighters got to their feet.

Muldoon winked. "Next round, darlin'."

Stone shuffled back to his stool. Slipchuck dabbed his face with a wet rag. "You're takin' a beatin', Johnny. I think you'd better lay down."

Stone breathed deeply. He had to dig into himself and bring something new and powerful out, because the fight was for Marie herself. If he languished two months at Fort Hays, she might be gone from San Francisco before he got there.

The bell rang, and Stone moved to the center of the ring.

Muldoon came straight for him, but he didn't try to dance out of the way. Muldoon uncorked a hook to Stone's side, but Stone beat him to the punch, snapping his head back with a left jab followed by an overhand right calculated to put him away. Both punches landed cleanly, but didn't effect Muldoon, who worked Stone's body in a series of punches and combinations that had no end.

Stone stood toe to toe with him, delivering swift shots, ducking, weaving, looking for openings. He slammed Muldoon in the nose, hammered his ear, got in closer, elbowed him in the eye; they butted heads; the crowd went wild. They expected a slaughter, but it was a real fight!

Stone didn't take a step back or move to the side. He had to show Muldoon he wasn't afraid of him. Powerful blows rocked Stone, but he planted his feet and hurled his bloody fists through every opening he could find.

It was like punching the mattress. Stone felt discouraged, but had to keep on. The only alternative was throw in the towel.

The soldiers were on their feet, the fight no longer a sure thing. Stone could see out his right eye, his left eye was half-closed. His nose and lips bled, was sure at least one rib was broken.

Muldoon didn't look any better. The last head butt opened a cut above his right eye, his nose shattered, face a bloody mask, mouth open, breathing hard. Stone could smell Muldoon's lunch in the middle of the ring, and Muldoon's punches weren't hard as before. He's tiring!

"Two!" shouted Sergeant Major Gillespie.

A flash knockdown, Stone perched on one knee in the middle of the ring. He looked at Muldoon, still dangerous. Go back to the original strategy and box him.

At the count of nine, Stone rose to his feet. Muldoon came at him like an angry bull, and Stone danced to the side, flicking out his left jab, catching Muldoon on his nose. Muldoon shifted direction, raising his hands to protect his head, and Stone smacked him in the pit of his stomach. Muldoon continued his charge, throwing a left hook at Stone's kidney, but Stone danced out of the way, throwing a three-punch combination to Muldoon's head and torso. Muldoon shifted direction, impatience and frustration on his face.

Stone winked at him. "I'm still here, darlin'."

Muldoon unleashed a vicious right hook to Stone's ribs, but Stone blocked it with his elbow, then the bell rang. A cheer arose from the crowd as both fighters returned to their corners.

Stone sat on his stool and drank water, energized by the knowledge that Muldoon was an ordinary man who got tired. Accustomed to knocking out opponents in the first round, he probably didn't train hard, Stone had survived his worst. The champion lay against the ringpost while his trainer massaged his belly.

I can be with Marie in a week if I'm strong in this round. Stone steeled himself for the ordeal that lay ahead.

The bell rang, and he came out dancing, hands held high. Muldoon rushed across the ring as expected, and led with an overhand right. Stone dodged, whacked Muldoon in the gut, hooked up to his head, went downstairs, leaned back to avoid an uppercut, and jabbed Muldoon in the mouth, then took a blow to his right kidney, threw one to Muldoon's left side, and Muldoon punched him in the mouth.

Stone decided to trick Muldoon, and fell back as if hurt. Muldoon rushed forward, his right hand dropped, and Stone put each of his two hundred forty pounds behind the bruised and battered bare knuckles of his right fist.

Muldoon faltered for the first time in the fight, but Stone didn't step back to assess damage or contemplate future strategy. He lowered his head and moved in for the kill, flinging his fists at Muldoon's body.

Muldoon took a step backward, and every man who bet on him knew it was a bad sign. The crowd became silent, awestruck at the sight of the champion on the receiving end for a change, but some men fight harder when they're hurt.

Muldoon couldn't give up easily, and reached inside for his remaining reserves. Stone hurled solid thuds into Muldoon's face, dodged Muldoon's punches, jabbed Muldoon's left eye, hooked him to the belly, threw a right cross at his ear, blocked a right cross, caught a hook on his bicep, landed an uppercut to the point of Muldoon's chin; Muldoon floundered.

Stone could barely see, his breath came in gasps, he pushed his man against the ropes. Muldoon fell backward, bounced; Stone cracked him in the mouth; Muldoon's legs wobbled. Muldoon raised his fists and massive hairy arms to protect his head and upper body; Stone smashed his belt line. Muldoon threw a jab at Stone's face, Stone wiped it away, landed a right hook to the side of Muldoon's head.

Muldoon went sprawling backward, his punches wild and erratic. Stone stayed on top of him, tasting victory. Lobo power crackled in his veins, he saw himself as an injun warrior with a feather sticking out of his hair. *I've got him!*

"Six!"

Stone lay on his back, his head spinning. He hadn't even seen the punch.

"Seven!"

He scrambled to his feet, tripped to the side. Muldoon snorted like a bull and charged, but was hurt and unsteady. The two fighters banged away at each other, dug shots into each other's ribs, butted each other with foreheads and elbows. Muldoon tried to poke a thumb into Stone's good eye, while Stone caught him with a hard right cross, threw an uppercut, then measured Muldoon with his left hand, while he loaded up with his right.

Stone drove his right fist forward with all his strength; Muldoon's legs buckled. He slammed Muldoon's face again and again, and the crowd watched in silence as the heavyweight champion of the Seventh Cavalry sank to his knees under the onslaught of the blows.

It was the first time Muldoon had ever been off his feet in the ring. The audience was thunderstruck. Sergeant Major Gillespie counted, while Muldoon struggled to rise like a bloody phoenix from the ground. Stone stood in a neutral corner, wiping blood out of his eye with the back of his hand.

Muldoon reeled in the center of the ring, blinking, wondering what had gone wrong.

"You all right?" Sergeant Major Gillespie asked him.

Muldoon grunted something unintelligble; Sergeant Major Gillespie stepped back; Stone tasted San Francisco. He grit his teeth and fired powerful punches at Muldoon, worked him up and down with jabs, hooks, uppercuts, mixing his attack. Muldoon desperately tried to cover and fight back, but he'd taken too many hard punches for too many rounds, and was wearing down.

He looked like a naughty little boy as he tried to hide behind his ham fists. Stone picked him apart methodically, fighting pity at the same time. When Muldoon raised a hand to protect his face, Stone buried a fist in his belly. When Muldoon tried to clinch, Stone stepped back and hit him with an uppercut.

Muldoon wouldn't go down. The crowd was silent, Stone's fists an unrelenting drumbeat. He wondered what he'd have to do to knock Muldoon out. He pawed with his left, ducked a lazy punch from Muldoon, cocked his right hand for the knockout blow. He saw the opening, let fly.

It rattled Muldoon to his toes, he sprawled backward onto the ropes, bounced, fell forward like a tree to the ground.

"One!" shouted Sergeant Major Gillespie.

Muldoon didn't move.

"Two!"

Stone shifted his weight from foot to foot as he stood in a neutral corner. At the count of eight Muldoon pushed himself to his knees, but his arms collapsed and he fell on his face.

"Nine."

Muldoon wasn't going to make it. Stone jumped into the air, and threw his fist at the sky. Slipchuck screamed like a maniac, he'd bet his entire poke at high odds, a rich man! The crowd watched dumbfounded as Sergeant Major Gillespie hollered, "Ten!" Sergeant Major Gillespie raised Stone's hand. "The winner, and *new* heavyweight champion of the Seventh Cavalry—*John Stone!*"

11

STONE WAS AWAKENED by the sound of shots. He opened his eyes and saw fellow passengers firing out the windows of the train. He turned to his right and saw a lobo streaking over the prairie, kicking up dirt.

The passengers shouted merrily, but Stone rooted for the lobo dodging and twisting for her life. She disappeared over the rise, and the passengers pulled their rifles in from the windows.

Stone sat in the rearmost seat with his back to the wall. A wood stove was bolted to the middle of the floor, radiating heat. The weather had turned cold; Stone needed a sweater under his fringed buckskin jacket. Pick one up in the next town.

The passengers closed the windows, the train rocked from side to side. Stone had been riding the rails since leaving Hays City early that morning. He and Slipchuck were on the way to San Francisco at last.

They'd said good-bye to General Custer and Libbie at the train station. Stone and the general spoke to each other in clipped sentences, made slim smiles, tried not to let their sadness show, as good friends came to a parting of the ways. They shook hands one last time; Stone and Slipchuck climbed aboard the train; it pulled out of the station and had been chugging west ever since, over the wide unchanging prairie. Stone dozed throughout the day, aching all over. He still felt the effects of the fight.

San Francisco in a week, depending on track conditions. He prayed Marie would be there when he arrived. Now at last he was hot on her trail. He took her picture out of his shirt pocket; she smiled at him, he felt good. They'd be together soon.

The door at the far end of the car opened; Slipchuck came into view, wearing a white frock coat, pants, stovepipe hat, and gold chain hanging over his belly, on his way back from the saloon car. He wavered from side to side as iron wheels rolled over iron tracks, producing a constant roar. Ladies raised their arms in alarm, afraid Slipchuck'd fall on them, but he made his way around the stove and dropped to a seat beside Stone.

John Stone's manager, trainer, second, and cut man closed his eyes and passed out. He'd been drunk since the end of the fight, spent all night in the hog pens, carrying on like a young man.

The train sped across the plains; Stone thought of his old friend Fannie Custer at Fort Hays, with his two principal subordinate commanders hating his guts, most of his men inferior soldier material, preparing for a major campaign against the injuns. It wasn't the prescription for success, but every man had to face his destiny, and even New York tycoons died.

Stone's sharp range-experienced eyes spotted a man on a far-off eminence. Probably an injun watching mystified as the iron horse crossed his ancestral lands, scaring away the buffalo. Stone felt his spirit go to the injun, and wished he could join him. In some strange part of his soul, Stone loved injuns. He raised his arm and waved, could swear the injun waved back.

The train jiggled and shook as it rumbled over the West Kansas plain. Stone wondered if injuns had got Tomahawk, and he was a war pony now. Or he gave himself up to some cowboy and was herding cattle, a task at which he excelled. He might've been killed by lobos, or maybe he was runnning free with a pack of wild mustangs. Stone hoped he'd see him again someday. Tomahawk was the best horse he'd owned in his life.

With shame, he remembered the fight with Bull Muldoon. He'd beaten the champion to a pulp, for the almighty dollar. Muldoon never did anything to him, and probably was a decent man. Stone felt as though he'd been through a sausage grinder. *I've got to stop fighting.*

The conductor, wearing a blue beetle suit and black visored cap, entered the car. "Bradshaw, next stop!" he announced. "Passengers departin', don't leave nothin' behind."

Men and women pulled down their bags from overhead racks. Stone figured they were nearing the border with Coloraddy. In two days they'd be in Denver, one of the wildest spots on the frontier.

The train slowed as it approached Bradshaw. Stone looked out the window, and saw the usual scattering of shacks. An old newspaperman said to Stone once: "You tell me the population of a town, I'll tell you what it looks like."

Stone gazed at the sun sinking low on the horizon. The train slowed, with longer intervals between chugs of the engine. Black cinders blew from the smokestack and covered everything with a fine ash. The engine came to a stop; Stone looked down the main street: saloons, a barbershop, general store, pawnshop, broken-down hotel. Passengers dragged their luggage to the doors.

The conductor held an excited conversation with a man in a suit in front of the train station, then walked resolutely back to the train. "Track damage ahead!" he announced. "Should be fixed in a few days! Silver Palace Hotel straight down the street! Sorry fer the delay!"

Stone groaned. Just when everything was going beautifully. He stuck his elbow into Slipchuck's ribs. Slipchuck opened his eyes and looked out the window.

Stone told him what happened. They pulled their saddlebags from the racks and followed the other passengers out the door. Stone stepped to the ground, a cinder from the smokestack landed in his left eye. He rubbed it with the back of his hand, corrosive coal smoke belching from the furnace of the train engine.

"Let's find a saloon," Slipchuck said.

The cool autumn wind whistled past Stone's ears as he walked onto the main street of Bradshaw. It was a dot in the middle of the plains, built to service the railroad, trying to grow and prosper deep in injun country, far from forts.

The third building down was the Blue Bonnet Saloon, and Slipchuck inclined toward it. A beggar on the sidewalk held out his filthy palm, and Slipchuck gave him a few coins. Stone pushed the swinging doors, and stepped out of the backlight, hands near twin Colts in crisscrossed holsters. A man in a derby tinkled a piano against the wall. Stone headed for the bar, spurs jangling with every step. Slipchuck came behind him, small eyes peering into the darkest corners, looking for enemies, card games, the best-looking whore in the establishment.

Stone rested his foot on the bar rail and spat into the big brass cuspidor nearby. Behind the bar was a painting of a woman reclining on a leopard-skin sofa, naked except for the diamond and emerald tiara binding her golden hair. Stone had to blink, because she looked something like Marie.

"What's yer pleasure?" asked the bartender, a bald man with long sideburns, wiping his hand on his dirty apron.

"You got any sarsaparilla?" Stone asked.

"No, sir, but we make root beer for fellers like you."

"A large glass, if you don't mind."

Stone heard a voice next to him roar: "Who's this galoot askin' fer baby water?" A man with a long lantern jaw looked contemptuously at Stone. "I don't drink next to sissies!"

Stone was about to say, *then get out,* when something at the far end of the bar caught his eye. It was an old Confederate cavalry hat, could it possibly be . . . ? Stone stepped around the man with the lantern jaw and walked toward the hat. The closer he got, the more familiar it looked, with the same dark stain on the left side of the crown. Then he recognized his shirt. Stone leaned against the bar, and examined the profile of the man wearing his clothes. Snead stood with one foot on the rail, staring into the middle distance. He'd beaten Stone, robbed him, and left him to die. Stone promised to kill him if he ever found him, saw no reason to change his mind now.

"Remember me?" Stone asked.

Snead turned toward Stone, and examined his face through narrowed eyes. Then Snead's jaw fell open, and he reached for a Colt. The barrel of Snead's gun cleared his holster, when Stone opened fire from a distance of three feet. The space between them filled with thick gunsmoke, shots reverberated through the saloon, and men dived to the floor.

Snead rocked back on his heels. He clasped both hands to his bleeding gut, stumbled to the side, and looked up at Stone, astonished by what had happened. One moment he was drinking whiskey, the next . . .

His mind blanked out, and he crashed into the floor at Stone's feet. Stone reached over and picked up his old Confederate cavalry hat. He inspected it carefully in the light of the coal-oil lamp. Pretty much the same. Stone removed the cowboy hat from his head, and put on his old Confederate calvary hat. A surge of electricity passed through him, and he felt like a young officer again. He pulled his old Apache knife out of Snead's boot and dropped it into his own, beside the Sioux knife. Then he strapped on his old twin Colts, glad to have them back again. A glass of root beer sat before him on the bar.

"You don't mind?" Stone asked the man with the lantern jaw.

"Not me," the man replied nervously, stepping backward.

Stone looked in the bar mirror, and was himself again. He raised the root beer to his lips, and drained the glass dry. It had no wallop, but slaked his thirst and washed the cinders out of his mouth. He turned, and looked around the saloon for a gun pointed at his back.

All eyes were on him. It was silent as a tomb. Nobody dared move. He might be a dangerous maniac who'd shoot them all. "Let's get out of here," he said to Slipchuck.

The ex-cavalry officer and ex-stagecoach driver walked toward the door, and everyone got out of their way. The strange pair stepped outside, and the saloon remained quiet for a few moments, then the bartender reached for a bottle and poured four fingers of rotgut.

"Anybody know who he is?" asked one of the patrons.

"Never seen him before," the bartender replied, "but he's got gunfighter writ all over him."

"Maybe he's famous," declared a gambler at the other side of the bar.

The bartender knocked back his glass, then refilled it with a shaky hand. "I never seen him before. Somebody better go fer the sheriff. Drinks on the house!"

The piano player pounded his keys as men crowded around the bar. The bartender filled their glasses. "Must've knowed each other. Wonder what it was all about?"

"Women or money," an old cowboy replied. "Ain't it always? Life don't mean much to them fellers. Always think they're a-gonna win."

They drank their toast as Snead lay in a pool of coagulating blood. Wind caused lanterns to swing back and forth from the rafters, and lobos could be heard howling on the distant prairie.

SPECIAL PREVIEW!

Introducing John Fury. Gunfighter. Legend.
Where there's trouble, there's . . .

FURY

Silent but deadly, he has no history and no home.
His only desire is justice.

Following is a special excerpt from this riveting new Western series—available from Berkley books . . .

FURY KNEW SOMETHING was wrong long before he saw the wagon train spread out, unmoving, across the plains in front of him.

From miles away, he had noticed the cloud of dust kicked up by the hooves of the mules and oxen pulling the wagons. Then he had seen that tan-colored pall stop and gradually be blown away by the ceaseless prairie wind.

It was the middle of the afternoon, much too early for a wagon train to be stopping for the day. Now, as Fury topped a small, grass-covered ridge and saw the motionless wagons about half a mile away, he wondered just what kind of damn fool was in charge of the train.

Stopping out in the open without even forming into a circle was like issuing an invitation to the Sioux, the Cheyenne, or the Pawnee. War parties roamed these plains all the time just looking for a situation as tempting as this one.

Fury reined in, leaned forward in his saddle, and thought about it. Nothing said he had to go help those pilgrims. They might not even want his help.

But from the looks of things, they needed his help, whether they wanted it or not.

He heeled the rangy lineback dun into a trot toward the wagons. As he approached, he saw figures scurrying back and forth around the canvas-topped vehicles. Looked sort of like an anthill after someone stomped on it.

Fury pulled the dun to a stop about twenty feet from the lead wagon. Near it a man was stretched out on the ground with so many men and women gathered around him that Fury could only catch a glimpse of him through the crowd. When some of the men turned to look at him, Fury said, "Howdy. Thought it looked like you were having trouble."

"Damn right, mister," one of the pilgrims snapped. "And if you're of a mind to give us more, I'd advise against it."

Fury crossed his hands on the saddlehorn and shifted in the saddle, easing his tired muscles. "I'm not looking to cause trouble for anybody," he said mildly.

He supposed he might appear a little threatening to a bunch of immigrants who until now had never been any farther west than the Mississippi. Several days had passed since his face had known the touch of the razor, and his rough-hewn features could be a little intimidating even without the beard stubble. Besides that, he was well armed with a Colt's Third Model Dragoon pistol holstered on his right hip, a bowie knife sheathed on his left, and a Sharps carbine in the saddleboot under his right thigh. And he had the look of a man who knew how to use all three weapons.

A husky, broad-shouldered six-footer, John Fury's height was apparent even on horseback. He wore a broad-brimmed, flat-crowned black hat, a blue work shirt, and fringed buckskin pants that were tucked into high-topped black boots. As he swung down from the saddle, a man's voice, husky with strain, called out, "Who's that? Who are you?"

The crowd parted, and Fury got a better look at the figure on the ground. It was obvious that he was the one who had spoken. There was blood on the man's face, and from the twisted look of him as he lay on the ground, he was busted up badly inside.

Fury lot the dun's reins trail on the ground, confident that the horse wouldn't go anywhere. He walked over to the injured man and crouched beside him. "Name's John Fury," he said.

The man's breath hissed between his teeth, whether in pain or surprise Fury couldn't have said. "Fury? I heard of you."

Fury just nodded. Quite a few people reacted that way when they heard his name.

"I'm . . . Leander Crofton. Wagonmaster of . . . this here train."

The man struggled to speak. He appeared to be in his fifties and had a short, grizzled beard and the leathery skin of a man who had spent nearly his whole life outdoors. His pale blue eyes were narrowed in a permanent squint.

"What happened to you?" Fury asked.

"It was a terrible accident—" began one of the men standing nearby, but he fell silent when Fury cast a hard glance at him. Fury had asked Crofton, and that was who he looked toward for the answer.

Crofton smiled a little, even though it cost him an effort. "Pulled a damn fool stunt," he said. "Horse nearly stopped on a rattler, and I let it rear up and get away from me. Never figured the critter'd spook so easy." The wagonmaster paused to draw a breath. The air rattled in his throat and chest. "Tossed me off and stomped all over me. Not the first time I been stepped on by a horse, but then a couple of the oxen pullin' the lead wagon got me, too, 'fore the driver could get 'em stopped."

"God forgive me, I . . . I am so sorry." The words came in a tortured voice from a small man with dark curly hair and a beard. He was looking down at Crofton with lines of misery etched onto his face.

"Wasn't your fault, Leo," Crofton said. "Just . . . bad luck."

Fury had seen men before who had been trampled by horses. Crofton was in a bad way, and Fury could tell by the look in the man's eyes that Crofton was well aware of it. The wagonmaster's chances were pretty slim.

"Mind if I look you over?" Fury asked. Maybe he could do something to make Crofton's passing a little easier, anyway.

One of the other men spoke before Crofton had a chance to answer. "Are you a doctor, sir?" he asked.

Fury glanced up at him, saw a slender, middle-aged man with iron-gray hair. "No, but I've patched up quite a few hurt men in my time."

"Well, I am a doctor," the gray-haired man said. "And I'd appreciate it if you wouldn't try to move or examine Mr. Crofton. I've already done that, and I've given him some laudanum to ease the pain."

Fury nodded. He had been about to suggest a shot of whiskey, but the laudanum would probably work better.

Crofton's voice was already slower and more drowsy from the drug as he said, "Fury . . ."

"Right here."

"I got to be sure about something . . . You said your name was . . . John Fury."

"That's right."

"The same John Fury who . . . rode with Fremont and Kit Carson?"

"I know them," Fury said simply.

"And had a run-in with Cougar Johnson in Santa Fe?"

"Yes."

"Traded slugs with Hemp Collier in San Antone last year?"

"He started the fight, didn't give me much choice but to finish it."

"Thought so." Crofton's hand lifted and weakly clutched Fury's sleeve. "You got to . . . make me a promise."

Fury didn't like the sound of that. Promises made to dying men usually led to a hell of a lot of trouble.

Crofton went on, "You got to give me . . . your word . . . that you'll take these folks through . . . to where they're goin'."

"I'm no wagonmaster," Fury said.

"You know the frontier," Crofton insisted. Anger gave him strength, made him rally enough to lift his head from the ground and glare at Fury. "You can get 'em through. I know you can."

"Don't excite him," warned the gray-haired doctor.

"Why the hell not?" Fury snapped, glancing up at the physician. He noticed now that the man had his arm around the shoulders of a pretty red-headed girl in her teens, probably his daughter. He went on, "What harm's it going to do?"

The girl exclaimed, "Oh! How can you be so . . . so callous?"

Crofton said, "Fury's just bein' practical, Carrie. He knows we got to . . . got to hash this out now. Only chance we'll get." He looked at Fury again. "I can't make you promise, but it . . . it'd sure set my mind at ease while I'm passin' over if I know you'd take care of these folks."

Fury sighed. It was rare for him to promise anything to anybody. Giving your word was a quick way of getting in over your head in somebody else's problems. But Crofton was dying, and even though they had never crossed paths before, Fury recognized in the old man a fellow Westerner.

"All right," he said.

A little shudder ran through Crofton's battered body, and he rested his head back against the grassy ground. "Thanks," he said, the word gusting out of him along with a ragged breath.

"Where are you headed?" Fury figured the immigrants could tell him, but he wanted to hear the destination from Crofton.

"Colorado Territory . . . Folks figure to start 'em a town . . . somewhere on the South Platte. Won't be hard for you to find . . . a good place."

No, it wouldn't, Fury thought. No wagon train journey could be called easy, but at least this one wouldn't have to deal with crossing mountains, just prairie.

Prairie filled with savages and outlaws, that is.

A grim smile plucked at Fury's mouth as that thought crossed his mind. "Anything else you need to tell me?" he asked Crofton.

The wagonmaster shook his head and let his eyelids slide closed. "Nope. Figger I'll rest a spell now. We can talk again later."

"Sure," Fury said softly, knowing that in all likelihood, Leander Crofton would never wake up from this rest.

Less than a minute later, Crofton coughed suddenly, a wracking sound. His head twisted to the side, and blood welled for a few seconds from the corner of his mouth. Fury heard some of the women in the crowd cry out and turn away, and he suspected some of the men did, too.

"Well, that's all," he said, straightening easily from his kneeling position beside Crofton's body. He looked at the doctor. The red-headed teenager had her face pressed to the front of her father's shirt and her shoulders were shaking with sobs. She wasn't the only one crying, and even the ones who were dry-eyed still looked plenty grim.

"We'll have a funeral service as soon as a grave is dug," said the doctor. "Then I suppose we'll be moving on. You should know, Mr. . . . Fury, was it? You should know that none of us will hold you to that promise you made to Mr. Crofton."

Fury shrugged. "Didn't ask if you intended to or not. I'm the one who made the promise. Reckon I'll keep it."

He saw surprise on some of the faces watching him. All of these travelers had probably figured him for some sort of drifter. Well, that was fair enough. Drifting was what he did best.

But that didn't mean he was a man who ignored promises. He had given his word, and there was no way he could back out now.

He met the startled stare of the doctor and went on, "Who's the captain here? You?"

"No, I . . . You see, we hadn't gotten around to electing a captain yet. We only left Independence a couple of weeks ago, and we were all happy with the leadership of Mr. Crofton. We didn't see the need to select a captain."

Crofton should have insisted on it, Fury thought with a grimace. You never could tell when trouble would pop up. Crofton's body lying on the ground was grisly proof of that.

Fury looked around at the crowd. From the number of people standing there, he figured most of the wagons in the train were at least represented in this gathering. Lifting his voice, he said, "You all heard what Crofton asked me to do. I gave him my word I'd take over this wagon train and get it on through to Colorado Territory. Anybody got any objection to that?"

His gaze moved over the faces of the men and women who were standing and looking silently back at him. The silence was awkward and heavy. No one was objecting, but Fury could tell they weren't too happy with this unexpected turn of events.

Well, he thought, when he had rolled out of his soogans that morning, he hadn't expected to be in charge of a wagon train full of strangers before the day was over.

The gray-haired doctor was the first one to find his voice. "We can't speak for everyone on the train, Mr. Fury," he said. "But I don't know you, sir, and I have some reservations about turning over the welfare of my daughter and myself to a total stranger."

Several others in the crowd nodded in agreement with the sentiment expressed by the physician.

"Crofton knew me."

"He knew you have a reputation as some sort of gunman!"

Fury took a deep breath and wished to hell he had come along after Crofton was already dead. Then he wouldn't be saddled with a pledge to take care of these people.

"I'm not wanted by the law," he said. "That's more than a lot of men out here on the frontier can say, especially those who have been here for as long as I have. Like I said, I'm not looking to cause trouble. I was riding along and minding my own business when I came across you people. There's too many of you for me to fight. You want to start out toward Colorado on your own, I can't stop you. But you're going to have to learn a hell of a lot in a hurry."

"What do you mean by that?"

Fury smiled grimly. "For one thing, if you stop spread out like this, you're making a target of yourselves for every Indian in these parts who wants a few fresh scalps for his lodge." He looked pointedly at the long red hair of the doctor's daughter. Carrie—that was what Crofton had called her, Fury remembered.

Her father paled a little, and another man said, "I didn't think there was any Indians this far east." Other murmurs of concern came from the crowd.

Fury knew he had gotten through to them. But before any of them had a chance to say that he should honor his promise to Crofton and take over, the sound of hoofbeats made him turn quickly.

A man was riding hard toward the wagon train from the west, leaning over the neck of his horse and urging it on to greater speed. The brim of his hat was blown back by the wind of his passage, and Fury saw anxious, dark brown features underneath it. The newcomer galloped up to the crowd gathered next to the lead wagon, hauled his lathered mount to halt, and dropped lithely from the saddle. His eyes went wide with shock when he saw Crofton's body on the ground, and then his gaze flicked to Fury.

"You son of a bitch!" he howled.

And his hand darted toward the gun holstered on his hip.